Zulfi is incensed. 'Sparky's right, you're nothing but a load of pedestrians!'

Joey's heroes fall silent and look at me. They're not impressed. Lee Jordan steps out of the shower, horribly naked, and nails me with his gaze. 'What did you call us?'

My heart thickens. I want to blurt out, *You don't frighten me*, but I'm scared, and so is Zulfi, I can tell you. Just the two of us in here – against five of them.

'I'm talking to you, you stuttering sparrow,' says Jordan. 'What do you mean, *pedestrians*?'

'Leave him alone,' says Zulfi. 'You're always picking on him.'

'What's the matter? Can't he talk for himself?'

'Yes I c-c-can!' I reply, and trying to forget the shooting pain in my leg, I hang a towel around my bird-frame and stand straight, conscious of another big moment, bigger than anything in the gym, because this is *real*, realer than football, and the real test is, can I stand up to these bully boys?

www.**books**at**transworld**.co.uk/childrens

THe BOTTLE-TOP KING

Jonathan Kebbe

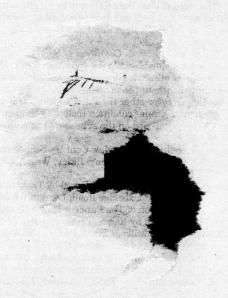

Corgi Yearling Books

THE BOTTLE-TOP KING
A CORGI YEARLING BOOK : 0 440 864674

First publication in Great Britain

PRINTING HISTORY
Corgi Yearling edition published 2001

1 3 5 7 9 10 8 6 4 2

Set in New Century Schoolbook by
Falcon Oast Graphic Art, Ilkley, West Yorkshire.

Corgi Yearling Books are published by Transworld Publishers,
61-63 Uxbridge Road, London W5 5SA,
a division of The Random House Group Ltd,
in Australia by Random House Australia (Pty) Ltd,
20 Alfred Street, Milsons Point, Sydney, NSW 2061, Australia,
in New Zealand by Random House New Zealand Ltd,
18 Poland Road, Glenfield, Auckland 10, New Zealand
and in South Africa by Random House (Pty) Ltd,
Endulini, 5a Jubilee Road, Parktown 2193, South Africa.

Made and printed in Great Britain by
Cox & Wyman, Reading, Berkshire.

To Bernie Payne
the lap-top King,
with thanks.

One

I like Mrs Okocha. It's like having an African queen teaching in our school. A smile from her and I go round in a daze for days.

She's starting a drama club, interested pupils invited to present themselves at lunch-time. I want to join, but do I have the nerve? When I get there the room's heaving with girls and boys waving arms.

'*Me*, miss – can I, miss? – I was first!'

I hover in the doorway. Slip away unseen. Maybe I'll be braver tomorrow.

I hate being me. Will I ever be able to walk into a room without blushing?

Next day I'm feeling better and return once more to Mrs Okocha's room.

'Hello, have you come about the drama? Don't be shy.'

I sit at the end of a row of perky hopefuls.

7

Why does everyone always look so confident?

'I want you all to think carefully about joining. Drama's tough and time-consuming. I'll need a letter from a parent giving you permission to stay after school . . .'

From *my* mum? I'm thinking – you must be joking.

We're asked to introduce ourselves. When it comes to me, I'm nearly stuck together with sweat.

'And what's *your* name?'

Ashamed of my stammer, I can only whisper.

She says, 'I'm sorry, I didn't quite catch that.'

Deep breath, 'L-Lewis, miss, Lewis O-Overfeld.'

The others giggle nervously.

'Lewis, tell me why you'd like to do drama?'

'My f-father's an actor and I think it's . . . I think it's in my b-b-b—'

I want to boast that acting's in my blood, but I'm too anxious to get the words out, and I can hear people thinking *Imagine having the nerve to come to drama when you can't even say your name!*

Mrs Okocha keeps me back a few minutes, rests a hand on my shoulder.

'Don't worry, Lewis; if you want to come to drama, you're more than welcome.'

I want to say, *No! I'm not making a fool of myself!* but all I manage is to mumble, 'Th-thank you, miss,' and run.

I'm grateful to Mrs Okocha for not making me feel bad. I wish she was my teacher instead of Mr Marvin.

'For heaven's sake, Overfeld, you're hopeless – what are you, Overfeld?'

'H-hopeless, sir.'

'You might as well be playing for the other side, you're a liability, Lewis – what are you?'

'A l-liability, sir,' I bleat obediently, when inside I'm thinking, for goodness' sake, this is only a wretched friendly against Mrs Okocha's class, not the bloomin' Cup Final.

'So take my advice, Lewis, when the ball comes to you, ignore it, keep out of its way, and whatever you do, don't attempt to kick it. Understood?'

'Yes, sir.'

'Why, Lewis?'

'Because I'm h-h-hopeless, sir.'

'Thank you!'

Everybody laughs and I laugh along to hide my shame.

He's not so bad, Mr Marvin, he just likes to win. If only he could see that I've a feeling for football, that I've the kind of mathematical mind you need to dissect defences or curve a ball into the path of a running teammate. I love the geometry of passing, the algebra of defence and counterattack, love seeing a well-crafted move lead precisely to a crisp goal. I hate those goalmouth scrambles where bodies pile in, the ball squirms over the line and everyone leaps around like they've won the Lottery.

I *know* I can play, but I've no confidence; I get flustered. I hate all that puffing and frenzy and players yelling at each other. I'm not someone who pushes and shoves. I queue politely at bus stops and hold doors open for old people and say things like 'After you'. But you can't say 'After you, mate' in the middle of a match. You have to get stuck in, I know that. But I'm not a get-stuck-in kind of person. If I bang into someone, I'm liable to say *Sorry!* which makes Mr Marvin mad.

'Lewis, why not offer him a tea cake while you're at it!'

'But, sir, I t-tripped him by m-mistake.'

'This is football, Lewis, not ballroom dancing! Get stuck in!'

I hate people shouting at me. I once got so upset in the playground I lashed the ball past my own keeper and stormed off in a huff. I'm a storm-off-in-a-huff kind of person.

It's hard being a wimp. I try and look relaxed when they tease me but I always go red. Mind you, apart from Lee Jordan, who gets a thrill out of tormenting me, the others don't mean any harm. They call me *pipsqueak*, *twit-face* and *swot* and I don't mind because I suppose that's what I am.

Or is it?

Sometimes, beneath the trembly exterior, I feel another boy bursting to get out.

I long for the nerve to tell jokes, long to stroll coolly into the drama club, long to make my parents see that I'm more than a good little boy. I love good films and imagine myself playing heroic roles. I love football and ache to express myself. I dream of being on the school stage and hearing classmates go, *Fantastic, Lewis, brilliant!* I dream of playing for the school, and Mr Marvin saying, *Great goal, Overfeld, didn't know you had it in you.* But all I ever get is, *Nice poem, very droll, Lewis,* or *Immaculate homework, gold star, you're an example to us all.*

Gold stars are nice enough – like I suppose what Dad feels when a whisky slips down his throat – and *You're an example to us all* warms my cheeks on a grey Monday morning, but if it's only for a column of fractions or a portrait of Saint Alban or an essay on the Great War, it hardly sets the blood tingling.

I yearn to break out of my fearful little cocoon.

I yearn to put six goals past Matthew Fallon.

Instead I trail home to my chores and homework and then, in the privacy of my room, where no-one can see, I lay out my five-feet by three-feet hardboard pitch with its painted touchlines, penalty areas and centre circle and get out my bottle-tops. I've been collecting for years. My mum's pleased I have a creative hobby but hates me going round with my nose to the ground hunting for suitable players, insisting on drowning them in disinfectant which has to be worse than any germs they might find in the gutter.

I have my favourites, like a gorgeous

Mexican beer bottle-top I found in Skegness and a scratched and dented Seven Up top discovered in the lining of a suitcase after forty years in an attic and a mysterious French one called *Maître Brasseur – GOLDHORN*, which could be a cider or a beer and has *pour ouvrir – tournez* around its serrated edge. I generally play eleven soft drinks tops against eleven ales and lagers from around the world, using my left hand against my right. My left hand is my team Middlesbrough, my right represents any of the big guns from Leeds to Lazio.

It's like Subuteo with bottle-tops. Using a finger, you flick players at a small plastic counter which serves as a ball, with goals cut out of tissue boxes. I play ten minutes each way with time added for stoppages, like when a player's sent off or rolls under the wardrobe. I'm left-handed, so although I'm nearly as good by now with my right, Middlesbrough usually wins, and if you happen to be passing my door you'll hear me going, 'And Lewis Overfeld gathers the ball on the half-way line – superb bit of control – rushes at the heart of the Juventus defence – quick one-two with Sparkling Perrier Water, side-steps two tackles, exchanges passes with Cidona and unleashes a terrific shot – oh my word, it's hit a post with Kronenburg in the Juve goal stranded!'

I go to bed on top of the world after leading Middlesbrough to another famous European trophy, and then lie there dreaming of tomorrow's games lesson when finally I'll burst out of my shell and amaze Joey and Winston and Lee Jordan, and of course Mr Marvin, with my remarkable dribbling skills and clinical shooting.

But when I wake in the morning, it's still me in the mirror. Mum says I'm handsome and have nice eyes and I'll have lots of girlfriends one day, but all I can see is a stammering twelve-year-old twit, always on the outside of things, a childish outline of a boy waiting to be coloured in. And when afternoon games arrives, and we jog round the pitch, I keep up quite well because I walk a lot and I'm fit. But when they're picking teams and I'm sticking out my chest . . .

'*I* don't want him.'

'Well *I* don't want him.'

'You have him.'

'No, *you* have him.'

My heart folds. All those sorry eyes on

14

me. Useless Lewis. The game starts and I put myself about and call for people to pass, but I'm ignored. The wind blows leaves across the pitch and I look up at the sky and wonder if there really is a God and all at once the ball's at my feet, a chance to display my wondrous gifts, voices shouting *Run with it! Pass!* or *Shoot!* or something, but in my fever to impress I stumble around like a clown, miskick, fall over myself.

'Oh Lewis, for God's sake!'

Useless Lewis, Hopeless Overfeld. What a name to be lumbered with. Why didn't my family change Overfeld to a legend's name or famous footballer? Then I'd be Lew Pacino or Lew Cruise, or Lewisfranco Zola, or Lew van Nistelroy or Lewy Floyd Hasselbaink! As it is, my name sparks merciless teasing. I try to sound cool by shortening Lewis to Lew, but then they go *Hey, Loo, remember to flush!* – Loo Overfeld: *loo overflowed!* – and everyone falls about. When I'm not being called Loo Paper or Loo Brush, I'm affectionately known as Lewis the Sparrow because I'm slight, quick and always twittering. Recovering my dignity, I brag about my dad but they soon tire of hearing about my famous father who's not that famous anyway – more theatre and radio-Shakespeare and the Classic Serial than soaps or TV dramas.

Only Mrs Okocha's impressed. 'I know him! Such a handsome man and such a fine actor. You *must* get me his autograph.'

Thrilled! 'I w-will, miss. Oh and miss . . . ?'

She turns, but I can see she's busy. Also she's new and they've given her 5C, a dreadful class full of loudmouths and nose-pickers, *and* she's in charge of the library, *and* I'm holding her up, and who'd want a twittering sparrow in her club anyway? When I open my mouth to speak, it comes out in a bumbling rush.

'M-miss, I was w-wondering if – if – if . . .'

'What were you wondering, Lewis?'

'If I m-m-might . . .' I want to say *try again for the drama club* but my throat's caught.

'Might what, Lewis? Take your time.'

'H-help tidy your l-library, miss.'

'I'd be delighted, Lewis, you are sweet.'

Nobody takes me seriously. I say, 'Dad, I think I'd like to be an actor like you s-some day,' and he ruffles my hair and says,

'Sure, why not?' which really means *I don't think so!*

'I'm serious, Dad, I w-want to be an a-actor.'

'Splendid. Great idea. Just don't tell your mother.'

On rare occasions when he's home, I'll say, 'Dad, can we knock a b-ball around in the p-park?'

And he says, 'I'm tired, Lewy, tomorrow.'

I plead with him. 'My brain needs o-oxygen and fathers are supposed to b-bond with sons, and anyway how will I ever l-learn about life if all I ever do is work, work, w-work?'

So we drive to the park because Dad's too lazy to walk, and he's suddenly enjoying himself, rediscovering old tricks, putting me in goal and blazing the ball past me like a school kid. And when I manage to persuade *him* to go in goal, he goes, 'God! The time, your mother will hit the roof!'

It's no good appealing to Mum – she has no time for anything but schoolwork and never tires of telling us how *her* education was neglected and how she had to do night school and re-take everything – but it doesn't stop me trying.

'Mum, I've a f-favour to . . . to . . .'

She fixes me with her gaze and I know it's hopeless.

'Mrs Okocha's s-starting a d-drama club after school, and I was—'

'*Drama?*' she says, like I said gun club or a glue-sniffing society.

'Drama's really g-good for you, Mum, it helps your s-self-confidence and might be better than s-speech therapy, so I was wondering—?'

'Can't she change it to a Saturday?'

'I don't think so, n-not just for me.'

'Then absolutely not. You know the rules.'

The rules, the flipping rules! She runs this house like a warship, every surface gleaming, everything in its place and everyone performing his duties. She works as a relationship guidance counsellor – putting couples back together again – and says she doesn't have time for arguments. Weekday evenings look like this:

4.15–4.30 discuss school day with Mum over bananas and cream to fatten me up

4.30–5.00 chores, like leaving out the rubbish or walking Rufus (our red setter, who recently

18

replaced our beloved boxer Boris, who I can't think about without crying)

5.00–5.30	tea (or dinner as Mum calls it)
5.30–7.00	homework in absolute silence
7.00–7.30	Mum checks homework and reminds me about the need to work, work, work! so I'll stay ahead of the pack, attend a top university and land a plum job in banking or computers. All very well, but when do I try things like drama and football? When do I *live*? *'There's time for all that when you're older,'* she says.
7.30–8.30	(except bath night) is free time for TV or bottle-tops
8.30–9.30	reading in bed

Nine-thirty sharp – 'Lights out, sweetheart! kiss kiss! Another big day at school tomorrow, sweet dreams.'

Sweet dreams indeed – lie awake more like, wondering will I ever amount to anything more than a swot?

TWO

One night my parents give a dinner party, and I'm trying to read under the covers when I hear giggling below and sneak out onto the landing and overhear snatches of jokes they're telling, and one of them, told by my dad, is really sick, just the kind they like in school – sicker even – about Julius Caesar and how it's his birthday. No-one knows what to get him cos he's tired of horses from Arabia and camels from Tunisia, gold this and silver that – until Mark Anthony says, *I got you something a little bit different*, and Caesar thinks *Ooh!* and perks up, and Mark Anthony says, *Close your eyes, my liege*, and leads him into the sunlight and says, *Now you may open them*, and Caesar opens them and blinks in amazement. As far as the eye can see, the avenue's lined with crucified Christians. Caesar's speechless and swoons down the avenue gazing into hundreds of pain-wracked faces, saying, *My dear friend, this is the best present ever* when suddenly they hear a far-off groan, and Caesar goes, *Listen! One of them's alive – how wonderful!* Off they run along the avenue, stopping to listen, until they find the groaning man high on a cross, desperate to say something before he croaks. *Quick, a ladder!* Caesar cries, and scrambles up to where the man is mouthing something, and says, *Come on, spit it out!* The man's eyes are wild, his mouth dry. Caesar calls for water, they fetch a cup and Caesar puts it to the fellow's lips, and the man tries again, murmuring desperately. *Speak up!* cries Caesar. *What are you trying to tell me?* And with one last effort the man fills his lungs and in the faintest voice whispers – wait for it! – *Happy Birthday to you, Happy Birthday to you, Happy Birthday, dear Caesar . . .*

And I'm thinking, this is the joke I've been waiting for, they'll die laughing – it even ties in with our Roman History project – and I'll be really popular. And this time I'll get it right, not like the last time – I cringe at the memory – a rainy lunch-time with everyone sitting around bored telling jokes, and I burst out, '*I* g-got one! What's the difference between a s-school and a l-lorry?' And they go, 'What, Lewis?' like they know it'll be feeble, and my confidence sags and I go, 'A lorry b-breaks up and a school breaks d-down!' And they look at me as if I'm a lunatic until Tessa Hacket takes pity and says, 'I think that was meant to be the other way round, Sparky.'

I remember dying inside, wishing I could turn into a woodlouse and scuttle away under a floorboard. I don't want that again, so this time I resolve to spend a whole week practising in the mirror until I can tell it confidently, smoothly and with barely a stammer. And I won't rush it, I'll wait for the right moment.

It comes one morning when Sir's called away and we're left to get on with our work and I pipe up, 'Anyone want to hear a brilliant joke?'

'No thanks, Flusher.'

'But it's a really grown-up one.'

Ah! That triggers some interest. Well, actually it doesn't.

'Honest, it's really s-sick, my m-mum hated it.'

'Go on then,' someone says and I take a deep breath, determined to project my voice like an actor – only instead I start shaking

22

like I just stepped out of the sea into a freezing wind. I've gone over it so many times, but never with an audience, and now they're all waiting to be shocked and in my anxiety to impress I rush in.

'W-well, you see, it's J-Julius Caesar's b-birthday, and he's in a h-huff cos everyone's b-bought him the usual s-slaves and chariots and things, until Mark Anthony says, *Well, actually, I've got you s-something a bit s-special*, and leads him out of the p-palace and – oh no! First he m-makes him sh-shut his eyes and then when they're outside he says, *Now, you can o-open them*, and Caesar o-opens them and gasps, *Oh my g-goodness!*—'

'Why, has he got a stammer too?' shouts Lee Jordan, and everyone laughs.

'No, because g-guess what, the avenue's f-full of—?'

'Strippers!'

'No, no, l-listen, it's really g-good, you see the avenue's lined on both sides with cr-cr-cr—'

'Cruise missiles?'

'No, n-no!'

'Cream doughnuts?'

'No, l-listen!'

'Christmas trees?'

'No, cr-crucified Chr-Christians . . .' That shuts them up. 'And Caesar's so pleased he gives Mark Anthony a big h-hug . . .'

'*Euugh!*' groans he-man Joey Spinx.

'And Caesar s-says, *Oh, thank you! Just what I always w-wanted . . .*'

'Is that it?' jeers Jordan.

'No, the b-best b-bit's to come, cos just then they hear a dis – a dis – a dis—'

'A disc jockey?'

'No, no, a—'

'A drippy little squirt called Lewis Overfeld,' laughs Lee Jordan.

'No, no!' Frantic now to reach the punch line. 'One of them's alive and Caesar calls for a ladder and climbs up and says *Speak up, I can't hear you*, but his m-mouth's dry and Caesar calls for w-water—'

'Oh for God's sake Lewis, get on with it.'

'OK, OK, so finally the man digs d-deep and says—'

Someone's in the doorway. I gape, open-mouthed.

'Says what?' enquires Mr Marvin.

I return his gaze helplessly.

'I thought I left you boys and girls to work in silence. And you of all people, Overfeld.'

'I'm s-sorry, sir, I'll get on with my w-work now.'

'Very noble of you, but first I want to hear what you had to say that was so vital?'

'We were talking history, sir,' my friend Zulfi says, trying to save me.

'Yeah, you know, the Romans, sir,' says Tessa Hacket.

'He was telling a joke, sir,' says honest Lee Jordan, 'and we're hanging on the punchline.'

'Lewis Overfeld telling a joke?' Sir is amazed. 'Well, well, we'll have to hear this.'

I try to wriggle out of it, but he insists I come to the front. It's all in a day's work to him, teaching a naughty boy a lesson, but for me to leave the safety of my desk and face the class is an agony.

'What do we want?' goes Joey Spinx.

'The punchline!' everyone shouts.

'When do we want it?'

'*Now!*'

'That's enough,' says Sir. 'Come along, Overfeld, up front and entertain us!'

What a fool I am! I jumped right into this, like one of those young men in 1914 who, having rushed to join up, found themselves glued to their trenches, petrified.

'Come on, we haven't all day,' says Sir like one of those officers drawing his pistol.

My heart shrivels up, I think I'm going to burst into tears. I get to my feet, mouth dry, face on fire.

'Sir, it's not fair,' Tessa calls.

'Nonsense!'

Others shout, 'We want to hear it, sir, don't we, sir?'

'We certainly do,' says Mr Marvin, 'and today rather than tomorrow.'

I sway, catch myself and I feel a rush of blood – *No! Absolutely not! I deserve to be punished, but not like this* – and I stand still in my place, head bowed, a deserter waiting for the bullet.

'He can't, sir, you know he can't,' says Zulfi.

'Course he can!' they cry.

'You get up and tell one if you're so clever,' Tessa challenges half the class.

Sir sighs, fixes me with a stern look, and to groans of disappointment lets me off with a hundred lines and a reminder in future not to tear off more than I can chew.

Miss Proudfoot, the principal, is as proud as her name suggests and she's not pleased with our football results and goes round

26

glowering at any senior boy who crosses her path. No-one else remembers, but Miss Proudfoot's forever recalling the Gerald Ashby Inter-Schools Cup we won – in *1979*! She tells us all about it at assembly – two goals down at the interval, four–two victors at the death – as though it happened last week, when no-one dares remind her that none of us were born then and half the teachers were in short trousers or playing hopscotch.

Miss Proudfoot can't bear to admit that Saley Marsh Middle School is nowadays pretty hopeless at nearly everything. Even now, half-way through the season, we're slipping like a leaking sub towards the foot of the inter-schools league, and she's livid. She's especially hard on poor Mr Marvin. Seated near the front, I distinctly overhear her growl one day when she comes into class.

'*Misss*ter Marvin, I'm frankly appalled by last Saturday's defeat, and against St Anthony's of all schools, and at *home*. It simply won't do. What *is* the matter? Don't we have any talent in school?'

'Indeed we do,' whispers Sir, pointing out Joey, Winston and Lee Jordan.

'Then why aren't we winning?'

'Well it's not that simple—'

'Oh yes it is, Mr Marvin. Work and inspiration is what's required. Work them harder and find ways to inspire them.'

'With respect, Headmistress—'

'These are bright children, Mr Marvin, perfectly capable of following the national curriculum *and* excelling on the playing field. Our results are an absolute scandal! I suggest you go home and have a jolly good think and come up with some pretty smart suggestions. And no excuses, Mr Marvin. I want results! What do I want, Mr Marvin?'

'Results, Miss Proudfoot.'

'Thank you!'

Sir pales. He's been spoken to like a naughty boy and there'll be hell to pay – and there is. He extends games lessons and puts us through gruelling circuits, sprints and press-ups and then expects heroics in our tragic mud-sodden matches, taking it out on anyone who fails to perform.

'Spinx, wake up, you oaf! – Call that a shot, Jordan? – Daley! That was more like a kiss than a tackle!'

'But sir, I'm not a natural defender.'

'You said it.'

And of course he picks on me. 'Overfeld,

this isn't Teddy Bears Playtime, get your hands out of your pockets. In fact, see me after.'

'What f-for, sir?'

'For not trying.'

'But I am, sir, it's just tha-tha-that—'

'Stop stammering, you imbecile and get stuck in!'

My cheeks burn. Lee Jordan laughs and mimics me, 'It's just *tha-tha-tha—*'

No-one else laughs. Sir shouldn't have said that, and knows it, and points a furious finger at Jordan. 'You! Round the pitch twice, and twenty press-ups!'

'I never said a thing, sir.'

'*Five* times round and *thirty* press-ups!'

'But sir, *you* started it.'

'*Ten* times and *forty* press-ups!'

Recklessly, as Jordan turns away scowling, I give him a smile of immense satisfaction and he flings me a look which says, *You're dead!*

Three

Sir's bright idea for improving standards is a five-a-side tournament in the gym at lunch-time. We're already committed to Miss Proudfoot's Sponsored Spelling Challenge (the world's most boring charity bash), and now Mr Marvin is seeking volunteers from the top two classes to opt for football as well, money earned from goals scored going to the same disabled children's charity.

'Boys like Lewis, you mean, sir?' murmurs Jordan.

Sir's proposal sparks a flurry of debate; who's to play in whose team and who will be left out? I think Mr Marvin would have been wiser to distribute players fairly – especially as even the girls can take part cos it's for charity – but he leaves it to us and we end up with two super teams, a cobbled-together staff team, and, *er* – Zulfi.

Zulfi Malik's a tall slim Asian boy with improbably long arms and legs who loves his football and is pretty good and complains bitterly because Sir ignores him.

'Please, sir,' he's forever saying, 'just give us a chance.'

'How many times must I tell you, Malik, the school team's picked.'

'But it's useless, sir,' Zulfi wails.

'What did you say?'

'Well, sir, two wins in seven matches.'

'And two draws. I don't think that's too bad myself. We've just been unlucky in front of goal.'

'Unlucky, sir? Spinx and Daley couldn't hit a house with a beachball.' You have to hand it to him, he's got guts. 'Try me, sir, I'm a natural, I won't let you down.'

He's not slow to brag either, which gets up Sir's nose.

'I've seen you, Malik, and if you're a natural, I'm Zinadene Zidane and your friend Sparky here . . .' jerking a thumb in my direction, 'is Pele.'

Gales of laughter all around, and Zulfi's wounded again, the hurt deeper each time, so that a once-bouncy happy boy skulks miserably round school. I feel sad for him. Zulfi's hot-tempered and a bit arrogant, but once you're his friend, he'll do anything for you. I'm his friend because we're both outsiders, eager to join in and always being left out, sometimes nastily by boys like Lee Jordan, who delights in whispering racist jibes in Zulfi's ear and then – after Tessa Hacket reports him – swears blind he never said a word. I'm not much good to Zulfi there; I don't dare say anything to Lee Jordan. The best I can do is support Zulfi's campaign to break into the team.

'Mr Marvin, s-sir,' I pluck up courage and knock, 'may I s-see you a minute?'

'Can't you see I'm busy?' he replies, not looking up from his lunch and marking.

Teachers are horribly overworked nowadays, not like in those old films where masters doze under mortarboards, rousing themselves occasionally to chalk an equation on the board.

'Sorry sir, but it's i-important.'

'All right, all right! What is it?'

'Well, sir, I really, r-really, r-really—'

'You really what, Lewis? My sandwich is growing mildew.'

'– think you should consider Zulfi for the school t-t-t—'

'Trip?'

'No, sir, the school t-t-t—'

'Treasure hunt?'

'No, sir, the school t-t-t—'

'Tongue-twisting tournament?'

I blush and turn away.

'Sorry! Sorry!' he calls me back. 'I don't mean to be impatient, child, it's just that – well, you would not believe the workload . . .'

'I know, sir, one b-blasted g-government after another.'

'Exactly. Anyway, come back here, you fool, I'm all ears.'

'Well, sir, I think you're being very sh-sh-short-sighted.'

Sir blinks.

'Zulfi's k-keen and skilled and a fierce comp-p-petitor and I believe he'd make a positive contribution to the t-team.'

'Do you now? How very interesting.'

'I'm s-serious, sir.'

'I can see that.' Mr Marvin puts down his pen and looks at me as if for the first time. 'But I have to question your judgement, Lewis. Your friend Zulfi may be keen and competitive and even skilful, but he's skin and bones. I need *lions* in my team, Lewis, not stick insects.'

* * *

Sir's five-a-side tournament presents Zulfi with a rare chance to put on a good show, and how he'd love to. But he has a *big* problem. No remaining talent is willing to join him. I hover hopefully but he doesn't notice. In desperation, he implores Tessa Hacket and Heather Jones to play, with Oscar Liedloff – more noted for his musical accomplishments – in goal where his broad hands and long fingers could come in useful, never mind he's never saved a shot in his life.

'Get up off your knees, Zulfi, for God's sake,' says Heather.

Some people laugh at the idea of Tessa and Heather playing, but why not? Tess may be better known for her dancing, but she supports Middlesbrough and her dad's brought her up no differently from her brothers, and you should see her in the playground when she's in the mood. As for Heather, she's big and rough and everyone's scared of her. The last time someone poked fun at her – Kenny Lunn called her a big lump – she shut his head in a desk and wouldn't let him go till he agreed to kiss her feet. It could be handy having a player who takes no prisoners.

Zulfi's agitated as we walk to the bus. 'I got Tess and Heather and Ozzy, but I still need one more – just one more player . . .'

'Just one more player,' I echo thoughtfully.

'*Where* am I going to find him?'

'I c-can't imagine, Zulf.'

All the time I'm praying that before the bus comes he'll notice me standing there and remember that I'm really quite useful. Or could be. Perhaps.

'One more player,' Zulfi groans, 'but who? Slowcoach Roche wouldn't mind, but the game's over before he's tied his laces. And Loopy Dewbury's well keen, but he's even smaller and scaredier than you. It'd be like asking Mickey Mouse to lead the Charge of the Light Brigade.'

Am I that small? That scared?

The bus sails into view. I say, 'You've a p-problem all right, Zulf, but there must be s-someone out there . . .'

We ride the bus in silence, Zulfi wrestling with his problem, me working up to suggesting that maybe, just maybe, he could do worse than pick me. But I'm proud. I won't beg and I'm terrified he'll laugh, so I resolve to say nothing – until his stop arrives and I think to myself, *This isn't fair – I AM good at football and if I don't say something now, it'll be too late and all I'll ever be is a solitary bookworm.* Before I know it I'm tugging his sleeve. 'Zulf . . .'

'What?'

'I was just th-thinking—'

'Quick, man, I got to go.'

'Maybe I know s-someone.'

'*What?*'

'For your t-team.'

The bus pulls up, people are moving, Zulfi calling down 'Hang on a sec!' and then over his shoulder as he stumbles down the stairs, 'Who, man, who?'

We're pulling away, I'm scrambling to the window, calling out with all my heart, 'Me, man, *me!*'

He catches himself on the pavement and frowns up, trying to read me, and feeling foolish, I grin, as much as to say *That's a good one, isn't it!* and he turns away laughing, tickled by my joke.

I sit down again, a stone in my heart. I thought Zulfi knew me. I thought he cared, but he only cares about himself. Sir's blind to Zulfi's talent, and Zulfi's blind to mine. I thought he was my friend.

I get sick that night. Even my no-nonsense mum's alarmed. I can't keep anything down and crawl into bed and turn my face to the wall, vowing never to look at a football again, never to watch another match on TV. I even resolve to bury my bottle-tops in the garden and never again lead Middlesbrough into Europe. Yes! I'm taking Sir's advice and when the ball comes to me, I'll jump out of its way and never, never, three times *never* kick a ball again as long as I live. And as for Zulfi, I'll talk to him out of politeness but our friendship is dead. In fact all friendship is dead, except with innocent animals like Rufus and Boris. Friendship's a sham like adverts and footballers' integrity, and I swear never to trust anyone again as long as I live.

In school next day I get on with my work and speak to no-one until Heather Jones looms over my desk and says, 'You OK, Sparrow? You look peeved.'

'I'm f-fine, thank you,' I reply loftily. 'It's just that I've discovered a sh-sh-shocking truth.'

Everyone looks at me. Heavens! That's a first. What shocking truth has Lewis Overfeld discovered? My tone and manner suggest something grave – a scandal in the staffroom perhaps, Mr Marvin and Mrs Okocha? Or Miss Proudfoot belongs to some weird coven?

'I've dis-dis-dis—'

'Discovered – discovered what, Lewis?'

I hate it when people fill in for me. I was about to announce grandly that I've discovered there's no such thing as friendship, and loyalty's a lie, and gratitude is the biggest fraud of all, but I clam up, denying them the benefit of my wisdom.

Even in his distracted state, running round looking for his fifth player, Zulfi finally notices how quiet I've gone.

'Hey man, what's up? You look like you swallowed a golfball.'

'I'm absolutely fine, thank you.'

'Don't brush me off, Sparrow. I know you, you're having a strop.'

'You don't know me!' I jump up and Zulfi jumps back and everyone gapes. 'N-n-nobody knows me, l-least of all you, Malik,' I cry, grabbing my things and stuffing them in my bag. 'I've h-had quite enough, I'm going h-home!'

'Hey, what's got into him?' Zulfi comes after me, catches me up in the playground.

'Did I say something? Do something? I didn't mean anything, man. I'm just so busy finding a player – you can't believe what it means to me – I really, *really* want to show Sir what I can . . .'

He stops mid-sentence, open-mouthed.

'Don't w-worry about me,' I say, striding on.

'I get it.' Running me down, tugging my sleeve. 'You weren't messing, were you?'

'I'm fine. I l-love being useless at everything but sums, poems and p-p-punctuation.'

'*Blast!*' Slaps himself in the head. 'How could I be so—? It's a *great* idea! You and me up front.'

'It's not a great idea. I'm h-hopeless.'

'You're not!'

'I am!'

'You're not!' Gripping my shoulders and shaking me. 'You just need a bit of confidence.'

'Admit it, Z-Zulfi, admit it.'

'I'm not admitting nothing.'

'You're just being nice.'

'I'm not being nice.'

'I'm f-fooling myself to think I could make a p-positive contribution.'

'Rubbish! You got bags of talent, you're just scared to show it.'

'That's the point, I'm s-scared.'

'Everyone gets scared, even me.'

'I'm t-ten times as scared, and that's why they're right. I'm a squirt, a wimp – p-pick me and it'll be like having W-Winnie-the-Pooh in attack.'

'That's cool. I want Winnie-the-Pooh in attack. In fact I *insist* on having Winnie-the-Pooh in attack.'

'But Zulfi . . .' Gazing helplessly at him, tears spilling over. 'I'm only a sparrow—'

'A brave sparrow – bravest sparrow ever!'

'OK, a b-brave one, but you'll be up against l-lions, you'll be m-massacred.'

Breaking into a grin Zulfi says, 'I already got a cellist, a dancer and Heather the Hulk in my team, so why not a sparrow? If we're going to be massacred, man, let's be m-m-massacred—' gently teasing me, 'in style!'

My heart soars, I dry my tears. Zulfi wants me in his team. All right, not much of a team, but somebody wants me, somebody wants *me*! I'm so happy, *so* happy, and who knows, maybe I will make a positive contribution, show the world I can play a bit too, shine like others shine.

'Great, that's sorted.' Zulfi sighs. 'You and me leading the line. Mighty Malik and Superwimp! They'll never know what hit them!'

FOUR

Days go by, and I'm so excited I can't sit still. I'm like a pup racing round the house with the lead in my teeth, impatient for the park.

Then reality strikes – things I've been avoiding, like the consent form lying unsigned at the bottom of my schoolbag. It's against the law or something for kids and adults to play competitive football against each other without parental permission – risk of injuries, I suppose. Even, normally, for girls and boys to play together, which I can understand, cos *I* certainly wouldn't like to face Heather Jones. So what do I do? It's no use giving Mum the form. I know what she'll say: 'Absolutely not! *My* education was ruined because I never had the opportunities you're getting, and I won't have this sort of thing distracting you from your studies . . .'

My only hope is Dad, but when am I going to see him? And anyway, even if he signs, what if it all goes wrong? What if I freeze in the fierce competitive atmosphere of a tournament and make a fool of myself? Lose the match for Zulfi?

And there's yet another problem. Zulfi wants us to start training after school, and at home-time he grabs us before any of us can escape. Tessa hates missing *Neighbours* but agrees to make an exception. Oscar has cello practice but says he'll wriggle out of it. Heather wants to go home.

'I don't need kicking practice.'

'You do, we all do,' Zulfi says. 'The gulf between us and them, man, is *massive*.' Spreading his spider arms to demonstrate the gulf. 'Wide enough to embarrass us all to death!'

'*Nah*, I'm not hanging round, I been in school all flaming day.'

'The park's not school, and this isn't about school – it's about pride, man, pride.'

'I'm not bothered.'

'You crazy, Jonesy, we need you,' says Zulfi. 'You're the rock of our defence.'

'Oh yeah!'

'Without you, man, we're a ship with no mast, a castle with no moat—'

'Yeah, yeah.'

'Knights with no armour, wire with no barbs, juggernauts with no jugger—'

'OK – OK!' Hands over ears. 'Just shuddup.'

'You'll play then?'

'*YES!*'

'*Cool!* Let's go. Couple of hours in the park and we'll be ready for anyone.'

'*Couple of hours?*' we all boggle.

'Well! Do you wanna get stuffed next week?' says Zulfi.

'We're going to get stuffed anyway,' says Tessa.

'Doesn't matter. Main thing is to make them sweat, earn a bit of respect.'

The word *respect* hangs in the air.

'What about Sparky?' someone reminds him, and for an awful moment I'm afraid Zulfi's forgotten me. But by his expression I see he's taken me for granted, forgotten my mum's rules.

'Oh yeah, nearly forgot, this is my new signing,' says Zulfi. 'Lewis *Renaldo* Overfeld, the other half of our attack! – What's wrong, Sparks?' I must have gone pale. 'You're not going to let me down?'

'I'd love to train with you m-more than

anything in the w-world, but my mum, she'd n-never – I mean—'

'You don't wanna bother about her,' says Heather, whose mum probably lets her booze and bop all night.

'You don't know his mum,' says Zulfi, screwing up his face. 'She makes Miss Proudfoot look like Mary Poppins.'

'Give her a call,' says Tess. 'Make something up.'

'I d-don't like lying.'

'It'll be a white lie,' she assures me.

'What's a white lie?' asks Zulfi suspiciously.

'One that does more good than harm,' says Oscar.

'She's not an easy p-person to lie to.'

'Tell her you got to help Mrs Okocha in the library,' suggests Tess.

'She'll exp-p-pect a note.'

'Tell her you got choir practice,' says Heather helpfully. We don't have a choir.

'I got it,' said Zulfi. 'Tell her we're all in detention cos someone nicked something and no-one owned up.'

'You have to give notice of d-detention.'

'Say you forgot to tell her.'

It's a good lie. I can't fault it. I'm trapped.

45

I've never lied to my mum. She'd be appalled.

While Zulfi goes to beg a ball from Sir – who's highly amused to learn the make-up of our team and makes Zulfi repeat it so he can laugh all over again – the others accompany me to a call box, and listen while I prepare to tell Mum the biggest whopper of my life. As I tap out the number, I rehearse in my head; *Mum, it's me – no, nothing's wrong, only I'm going to be late because we're all in detention – Yes, I know I should have told you, I'm sorry I forgot – I'm really sorry . . .*

She's home, she answers; I swallow and recite my wretched lie and say sorry over and over, and she says, 'All right, but do try and remember next time, and hurry home afterwards,' and I replace the receiver with a sigh and stumble out of the box to back-slapping congratulations – you'd think I'd done something wonderful like solve world hunger – and off we trot to the park, the worst team in the world out to earn respect, everyone in merry mood but me. I've just told my mum a walloping fib. Perhaps I should feel liberated, but I feel sick.

The park is wide open to the sky, my

heart aches for joy. Tessa shows us warm-up stretches and then, assuming a stern professional pose, Zulfi has us running round dribbling and passing and practising one-twos and cunning moves before gathering us round for an in-depth psychology lecture. 'Now listen, lads . . .'

Heather clears her throat sharply.

'And lasses,' Zulfi corrects himself.

'Lasses? What is this, *milk the cow*?'

'Well, what *are* you then?'

The girls confer.

'Beasts!' says Heather.

'Amazons!' says Tessa. 'Or since we're daring to break into a boy's sport, why not *sisters of the revolution*!'

Everyone laughs, and for a moment I forget my worries.

'Oh, terrific!' Zulfi applauds. 'That'll be handy in the gym when I have to shout, *Close 'em down, sisters of the revolution!*'

'Why not just call everybody *players*?' says sensible Oscar.

'As I was saying,' resumes Zulfi, 'before these amazons interrupted, Joey's men may be more experienced than us, and in theory should skin us alive, but we do have one massive . . .' spreading his telescopic arms again, '*massive* advantage.'

'Oh yeah?' says Heather.

'Yes! We're the surprise package of the tournament.'

'In what way?'

'Nobody's ever played us.'

'That's because *we've* never played anyone.'

'Exactly! So they won't know what we're capable of, or how we're going to come at them.'

'Wow, yeah, that's a *massive* advantage,' says Heather.

'Overwhelming,' says Oscar.

'We can't lose!' cries Tess.

I lose track of time. I'm enjoying myself, one of the gang, running and passing and laughing at Zulfi for taking it so seriously.

Mists roll in, night's falling. Suddenly, *Oh my God!*

'B-bye, everyone!'

'Hey, Sparky, what's up?'

Running, running – hopping up and down at the bus stop, sick with fear – willing the bus to hurry! hurry! Panting through the broad crescents of our neighbourhood, every street an eternity, heart rattling, legs and lungs howling for relief. *Keep going. Keep going!* all the time wishing Dad was home to keep Mum from going bananas.

Gasping for breath, I turn the key in the door and fall into the hall to meet my mother's gaze. I've never seen that look before.

'Where have you been?'

'S-school, Mum, I told you I'd be—'

'Late, but not this late?'

'It was rather a l-long detention.'

'It's pitch dark for goodness' sake—' Rufus is going berserk, trying to lick my face. 'Rufus! *Basket!*' My mum flaps her arms at him and he bounds away and she starts again, 'You've never been this late – I couldn't think what could have happened. I was going to call the police—'

'Mum, c-calm down, please.'

'You've no idea the worry you caused me. Detention couldn't have finished later than four-thirty or five and you know what time it is now?'

'Mum, I'm sorry, I didn't r-r-r—'

'Your sister's distraught, I've never *seen* her so upset – I hope it wasn't that woman's drama club?'

'No, n-no.'

I can see Lindsay peeking red-eyed

through the banisters, her whole world rocked by my irresponsibility.

'Are you telling lies, Lewis?'

'L-lies?'

'Because you know it's the one thing I won't stand for.'

'N-no.'

'Well then, what?'

Whispering, 'F-football, Mum.'

'Because whatever it is, I want the whole—' She was going to say *truth* but whips off her specs and gazes at me. 'What did you say?'

The house falls still, Lindsay on the stairs, Rufus under the hall table, Mum regarding me as if I've just confessed to some heinous unsolved murder, her specs held out like handcuffs.

'Football? What do you mean, football?'

'I lost t-track of t-time. I was having . . .' *So much fun*, I meant to say, and she's read it, because she's coming at me hands raised, and I'm thinking, *Oh my God, she's going to hit me for the first time in my—!* and I flinch like a dog and shut my eyes . . . only to feel her arms around me, drawing me in, a rare thing in our house, my face wet with her face.

'You're safely home now, that's all that

matters. Don't worry about chores, everything's done. Do your homework and come down for supper.'

Just before lights out, still shaking, I take out my bottle-tops for the comfort of feeling them and spread them over the duvet, trying to decide whether to play Fiorentina or Bayern Munich tomorrow against mighty Middlesbrough.

five

My Aunt Sophie's house, my gran's seventieth birthday. Normally I enjoy these gatherings, but I've got myself into a state because I'm supposed to be going round asking people who've sponsored me for the spelling challenge to pledge their money to the soccer tournament too (the vague sponsor form just said *'charitable contests'*), but I daren't in case Mum finds out. I suppose I could play for Zulfi and still take the spelling tests – *if* I can get this rotten form signed.

Dad's supposed to be dropping by – he's doing a radio recording in Durham, not a million miles away – and the consent form lies in my back pocket, warming my bum, just in case.

My hated cousin is here. Everyone says he's brilliant – only fifteen and already tipped for Oxford or Cambridge – and

Gran's forever saying things like, 'Look at Carl, how hard he works, how well he's doing. *He* doesn't have film stars on *his* wall!' and I want to say, *I work just as hard, Gran – I can't help it if I'm not as brainy*.

The evening drags. No sign of Dad; he's going to let us down again. I'm too hot in my jacket but Mum frowns horribly when I mime across the table, *May I take it off?* You'd think I was asking permission to take *everything* off! When she's not looking, I loosen my wretched tie – what's the point of them anyway? They don't *do* anything. Whoever invented ties, I'd like to wind mine around his neck and—

Dad! He's just walked in, shaking the rain from his hair, smiles for everyone, everybody's favourite flatterer, handsome in a casual kind of way, half sincere, half *acting*. Kisses Gran, kisses Aunt Sophie – leaning back to admire her – kisses Mum, kisses people he hardly knows, kisses Lindsay, winks at me. I help clear the table, floating through all the chatter and cigarette smoke, looking for an opportunity to grab Dad, which is impossible since he's entertaining everyone at once, packing every minute with interested facial expressions and cheery nonsense before he rushes back to wherever he's staying tonight. Mum's forever saying, 'If only your father had used his superb brain when he had the opportunity, he wouldn't be charging round the country doing bits and pieces to make a living.'

But some people follow their hearts, I want to tell her. *Some folk choose fun before money.*

Ah! I see my chance. Mum's in the kitchen whispering with poor Aunt Ruth – even off-duty, she mends marriages – and Dad's taken his coffee to the far end of the table to sit beside Granddad, and to be nearer the door for a quick getaway, so I follow, checking the coast is clear before sliding the consent form under his elbow.

'S-sorry, Dad, to inter-r-r-r . . .'

They're passionately talking football, which is funny, because Dad couldn't care less about football and wouldn't mind in the least if Germany or Malta or the Isle of Skye beat England five hundred nil. 'It's OK, Lewy, what is it?'

'N-nothing important, D-dad, just a f-form to sign, a charity thing.'

'No problem, mate.'

Hold the pen out. He doesn't see it. Tap lightly on his hand as he natters with

Granddad, but he doesn't feel it. Slip the pen into his hand, close his fingers around it.

'No h-hurry, Dad . . . sometime before Easter would be f-fine.'

He scrawls his elegant autograph, doesn't even look at the form. It could have said, *I the undersigned agree to hand over all my worldly goods, golf clubs, beer mat collection and money to my son Lewis, my daughter Lindsay and my dog Rufus.*

Sometimes I wish my dad cared a little bit more, and my mum a little bit less.

Six

The big day has arrived. Everything's set up in the gym, the four teams marked up on a big blackboard by witty Mr Marvin. Team A, the *All Stars* – pick of the school team – looks like this:

Joey *the King* Spinx (Capt.)
Kenny *Slicker* Lunn
Winston *Calypso* Daley
Lee *Psycho* Jordan
Matthew *the Eagle* Fallon (goal)

Wait a minute! There's something funny here. That's not all Mr Marvin's writing. Someone's added those nick-names – someone with neat writing, egged on by his mates – and look how chuffed they are with their hard-man nicknames, ribbing each other and laughing about how they're going to murder everyone, especially us.

Team B, led by Marc *Chopper* McCall

and calling themselves *the Jackals*, boasts five lesser mortals from the First Eleven.

Team C is a hilarious staff team composed of Mr Marvin, Miss Scott (our music teacher), Mr Grimes (our grisly chain-smoking caretaker), Bruno (his dinosaur son) and – would you believe it? – Mrs Okocha!

And finally there's Team D, chalked up for all to see, with nicknames *we* certainly didn't pick;

Zulfi *the Stick Insect* Malik (Capt.)

Heather *the Tank* Jones

Tessa *the Hips* Hacket

Lewis *the Sparrow* Overfeld

Oscar *the Fiddler* Liedloff (goal)

And the *Improbables* – as Mr Marvin has christened us – has been crossed out by some comedian and replaced with *the Girlywimps*.

Zulfi's eyes nearly hop out of his head. He can just about live with *Stick Insect* Malik and *the Improbables* – but *Girlywimps*, never! And Heather, disgusted at seeing herself described as *the Tank*, and even more incensed by *Girlywimps*, kicks up an awful row.

'Sir, that's disgusting! I'll kill whoever wrote that.'

Sir merely laughs, says she can't take a joke.

'We'll see about this,' Heather vows darkly, and glowering at everyone, grabs the chalk, rubs out *Girlywimps*, ponders a moment and scrawls *Invincibles* instead, then alters her title from Heather *the Tank* to Heather *the Hit Man* Jones.

Now Tessa snatches the chalk, rubs out *Hips*, and in her immaculate script replaces it with Tessa *Shooting Star* Hacket, and looks round triumphantly.

Oscar doesn't mind being called *the Fiddler*; he just shrugs. And I'm used to be being called *Sparrow*, so I leave it too. Just to see my name up there in a team called *the Invincibles* makes my heart beat wildly . . . until my terrors return to claim me, murmuring darkly, *You're not up to this, Lewis, you're going to make such an ass of yourself.*

I feel ill.

It's a simple knock-out competition. We're drawn against the teachers. What a laugh! With nerves jangling we sit out the first match, Joey *the King*'s All Stars clashing with *Chopper* McCall's Jackals and overcoming them five–four in a keenly fought game.

Now it's our turn, and the crowd cheers as Team C appears, Sir in flashy new trainers and best Leeds United strip, and lithe Miss Scott hopping up and down in shiny shorts and fetching tank top; and the school's villainous-looking caretaker Mr Grimes prowling in overalls, and Bruno, his immense son, bulging out of a faded blue boilersuit; and finally bare-footed Mrs Okocha peeling off to reveal a gold and purple tracksuit, setting off her glowing skin.

When we step in the open, we draw nothing but laughs. The Invincibles indeed! We must look a sight: gangling Zulfi in his floppy shorts and tattered *Kluivert* shirt; slender Tessa in bicycle shorts and leg warmers; hefty Heather in a ghastly blancmange tracksuit and size nine trainers; pale quivering me in my wildly expensive designer sweatshirt with its silly teacher's tick logo; and finally Oscar, in an old pair of cords and T-shirt, scratching his head and exploring his goal like someone who's never seen a goal before and wonders what it could be.

We watch as the opposition, typically efficient teachers, organize themselves for kick-off. Jaunty Mr Marvin, undergoing rigorous leg stretches, has put himself in midfield to direct play, with Miss Scott, in whom he obviously has faith, looking nimble but nervous up front, and Mr Grimes and Bruno making up a kind of Maginot Line in defence. The resplendent Mrs Okocha is in goal. Is there any chance of beating them? we ask ourselves, and we're probably thinking, *Yes!* when to our dismay we see who Sir has picked to referee the match. Himself!

'That's not fair,' my teammates object, but he's having none of it, indignantly waving them away, threatening to yellow card them before the match has even started!

'I trust you're not inferring I'm not capable of playing on one side and ref-ereeing fairly?'

Well yes, actually, that's precisely what we're inferring, but no-one dares say it, except with looks we exchange as we take up positions.

'Right lads! – and sisters of the revol-ution!' Zulfi claps his hands and looks encouragingly round at us. 'Remember what I said. Surprise packages win respect!'

Tess and Heather roll their eyes, but I'm inspired. Respect – *yes!* That's what we want.

Zulfi and Sir come face to face. Sir produces a coin and says, 'Call,' and Zulfi calls 'Heads! No, tails! No, heads!' and Sir says, 'Make your mind up, for heaven's sake!' and Zulfi, ever superstitious, cries, 'OK then, heads! – no! *Yes!* Definitely heads!' and Sir tosses the coin high, and down it comes with a smack, and Sir sighs regretfully, 'Tails it is! I'll kick off. Happy with that end? Good, let's go!'

While Zulfi turns dizzily away, Mr Marvin jogs over to each of his players to whisper final instructions. He's all pumped up and swanky, obviously taking this very seriously and my heart wobbles. Competition is so much scarier than the dreamy bottle-top campaigns of my bedroom. This is real life, me in a real team against grown-ups before a live crowd, with every risk of playing like a clot and letting my side down. Alone with my bottle-tops it doesn't matter if my left hand has an off day. But here, in front of everyone . . .

You're gifted! I tell myself. All you've got to do is *relax*, and set your talent free.

But how? How do you let go? I'm thinking, queasy with fear, of all those shaming looks when I screw up, looks that will follow me for days and last for ever. And as we wait for kick-off, I watch Sir synchronizing his watch, and Miss Scott with her ponytail and tennis star's headband, jogging on the spot, and mean-looking Mr Grimes rubbing his hands in anticipation of a good scrap, and his monstrous son hopping from one foot to the other making the floor shake, and Mrs Okocha doing a little African jig in goal. To settle my nerves I quickly calculate that their combined age must be in the region of a hundred and seventy-five.

I look at my teammates, seeking comfort in *their* anxiety, only to see them looking remarkably focused. Tessa is bending her legs and twisting her neck like a professional dancer, Heather is hunched forward, hands on hips like a bull, and Zulfi, slick with worry, is sprinting on the spot. Away on his own Oscar is packing away his glasses for safe keeping and staring out of his goal like a suspect in an identity parade.

Then I catch sight of Joey's All Stars leaning back to watch the fun, waiting to destroy the winners of this pantomime, and I meekly return *Calypso* Daley's sunny smile which goes something like, *Good luck, Sparks, you're going to need it!*

Then I find myself meeting Lee Jordan's gaze which is not half as friendly and promises to eat me alive.

Now Zulfi's running over to drag me into a central position, hissing, 'Go for Sir and Miss the moment they kick off.'

Placing a bright new ball on the centre spot, Sir checks his watch, flourishes a whistle and gives a piercing blow, and Oh God, we're away! and I'm instantly overwhelmed by the rush of play as Mr Marvin hurtles past me, knocks Heather flying and shoots so hard that Oscar never sees the ball and still isn't sure what happened after it smacks his crossbar and rebounds the length of the gym, straight to the feet of a grateful Zulfi, who swivels on one long complicated leg and sweeps it past a mesmerized Mrs Okocha.

Teachers Etc. *nil* – Invincibles *one*!

The crowd *gasps*. The game's barely fifteen seconds old and the no-hopers have the lead! Even Zulfi can't believe it, twisting his neck in Sir's direction for confirmation that he did just score, which

Sir duly announces with a faint begrudging puff on his whistle.

Away we go again, all huff and running, and still I can't engage, can't comprehend the speed of events, the lack of breathing space to look up and calculate a move. Everything's in motion, people flying by shouting at each other, shouting at me, the crowd shouting encouragement to heaven knows who and laughing as the ball bounds this way and that, and bodies slip and trip and tumble, and then an ironic cheer goes up, the teachers are withdrawing in orderly fashion and Zulfi's holding his head so I know the opposition's scored, and I know by Mr Marvin's smirk and Miss Scott's fervent congratulations that Sir is the hero.

Teachers Etc. *one* – Invincibles *one*.

'For God's sake, Lewis,' Zulfi snarls as we prepare to restart, 'get stuck in – this is serious. We can win.'

I shoot him a wounded look. He says, 'Don't look at me, you're the one standing there like an egg. Run home to your bottle-tops if you don't want to play.'

The gym spins around me, Zulfi goes out of focus and someone – Tessa I think – brushes me aside to take the kick-off and

64

the mayhem begins again, and all I can see is me turning away and running from the gym, down the corridor and through the fire door into the open air, the car park, the back lane and the bus stop. Home, the safety of rules and routine, and Orangina leading Middlesbrough out into the San Siro Stadium . . .

Then an *Oooo!* from the crowd startles me, and looking round I see I haven't moved, I'm still in the gym where Miss Scott is frowning after stinging Oscar's hands with a shot, and then everything's in motion again, players panting and grunting and banging into each other, rubber soles squeaking on the slippery floor and cries of 'Here, Ozzy!' – 'Mark her, Mr Grimes!' – 'Down the wing, Tess!' echoing off the walls, and now someone's calling me, drawing my attention, Tessa planning to pass to me, probably cos no-one's bothering to mark me, and oh God the ball's coming! A smooth pass to my feet taking for ever to cross the floor towards me, and as I watch, I spot Sir in the corner of one eye charging like a rhino, and in the other Mr Grimes rushing me like an assassin, and torn between longing and terror, self belief and surrender, I react, I simply react, and the next thing I know I'm meeting the oncoming ball, reaching it just in time to toe-poke it clear of Sir's outstretched hoof, and in the same breath jab it through the caretaker's legs into the path of screaming Tess, who takes it in her stride and shoots ferociously at goal – the ball striking Mrs Okocha's arms and falling to Zulfi who tucks it gleefully under her.

The crowd bursts into applause.

Teachers Etc. *one* – Invincibles *two*!

You can catch the buzz of disbelief around the gym as Zulfi applauds Tess and dashes over to whack me on the back, nearly flooring me.

'That's more like it, man!'

And here's Tess, running up to wave a fist in my face and shout *'Yes!'*

Even Mrs Okocha's clapping, earning a harsh look from Mr Marvin, who's anxious to get on with it and doesn't appreciate his goalkeeper's sportsmanship.

My head spins. I've laid on a goal for my teammates – *me*, Lewis! I'm shocked, light as air, the blood popping in my head, and now *I'm* chasing the game, daring to make myself available, and all at once I feel a nip of freedom, an exquisite pain in my side as I collect a loose ball, skip away from lumbering Bruno and send a clean diagonal pass behind retreating Mr Marvin into Zulfi's galloping feet – *wham! Goal!*

Oh yes! The crowd erupts. *Super!* So super that Sir can only gaze at his goalkeeper, a look which Mrs Okocha, getting off her knees, answers with a merry shrug, as if to say, what could I do? And anyway, it's only a game!

Only a game? Don't tell Mr Marvin.

Teachers Etc. *one* – Invincibles *three*!

We're off again, four minutes left, Sir shouting at Miss Scott, yelling at Mr Grimes, bellowing at Bruno, urging his troops to greater effort – Zulfi pleading the same from us – and then, just when Zulfi thinks victory's in the bag, Sir roughly dispossesses him, exchanges passes with Miss Scott, and is about to unload an unstoppable shot at cringing Oscar when *Hit Man* Heather slides wildly into him – *WHAM!* – not so much a tackle, more a road-accident, and not so much an accident, more a deliberate ramming, sending him sprawling into the penalty area, the full weight of her fall catching him in the head for good measure.

He lies on the floor perfectly still. The

crowd holds its breath. I fear – some of us hope – he's been knocked out, but assisted by Mrs Okocha and Miss Scott, he's on his feet, rubbing his head, stopping his watch and summoning Heather with a curling finger.

Zulfi complains hotly but it's no use. Heather's dismissed to a chorus of boos and cheers and Mr Marvin prepares to take the kick himself. Did Heather foul him *inside* the area? Zulfi thinks not but clams up when Mr Marvin threatens to send him off as well. Placing the ball, Sir looks up and squints at Oscar, who stares out in his goal like a deserter into the eyes of a firing squad.

Bang!

Teachers Etc. *two!* – Invincibles *three*.

Mr Marvin's in a sweat. We're a man down – a player down, I should say – and vulnerable, so he still thinks he can win. Time is crucial – there can't be much left – and Tessa politely reminds him to restart his watch.

But even outnumbered we're scarcely disadvantaged. We're lean and young and not yet ruined by smoking, whereas Bruno and Mr Grimes are like two hunted beasts running out of puff, leaving Miss Scott and Sir to do the chasing, and with the clock ticking down the final minute and the crowd chanting *'Twenty-seven, twenty-six, twenty-five . . .'* Sir yells at Mrs Okocha to abandon her post, a promising gamble at first as she joins the attack with fresh and surprisingly agile feet – until Sir is surprised by a simple tackle from Tess, her elegant dancer's foot darting in to nick the ball and flick it away where – after a moment's terror – I seize on it and set off for Mrs Okocha's deserted goal.

Of course I hear them coming – tireless Miss Scott and frantic Mr Marvin – but no force on earth is going to catch me now and, urged on by the crowd, Lewis *the Sparrow* Overfeld runs the length of the gym to slide the ball home.

Gales of laughter lift the roof.

According to the clock, the game's long over, but Sir won't hear of it.

'Injury time! Or have you forgotten I was poleaxed just now? Two minutes.'

'Two minutes?' Zulfi aghast.

'Half a minute at most,' Tessa cries.

'It was two! – I timed it.'

No use arguing. 'Come on, lads and

sisters – I mean *sister* – of the revolution,' Zulfi implores us. 'One last effort!'

He needn't worry. Mrs Okocha – back in goal – calls encouragingly downfield, but Mr Grimes and Bruno can only stagger round like mortally wounded buffaloes and Miss Scott's still full of running but the zip's gone out of her, and even Sir's bounding about with his tongue flapping like a hound in summer, while the crowd chants, 'Time's up, time's up!'

Mr Marvin, after what seems an eternity, blows in surrender.

We've won! *We've won!*

My heart somersaults. What a feeling! What bliss! Not because we've beaten the staff, but for accomplishing what none thought possible. The jokers have played like kings and queens – the losers have won! And for me it's a personal earthquake, my old life flung in the air, joy raining down. I've finally crawled – no! – *leapt* – from my timid cocoon and *shone*! The sparrow has landed! For once in my life I'm a hero. Zulfi's hotchpotch team are all heroes, and when the whistle goes we punch the air and throw our arms round each other in a spontaneous display of camaraderie.

Well, actually, we don't. We stand dazed and apologetic, too drained and embarrassed to celebrate. And even in our moment of glory, we sense trouble. The crowd may be cheering and Zulfi may have a jig in his hips as he walks off but the All Stars are waiting for us.

'Enjoy your little win,' laughs Joey, 'cos tomorrow we're going to bury you.'

'And it won't be a pretty sight,' Winston laughs.

'Yeah, and guess who's marking you, Flusher?' Lee Jordan grins.

A shiver goes through me.

Back in class, Sir makes us work in deathly silence. He's taking it badly, losing to an inferior pupils' team. But it's not Sir I'm worried about. I breeze through the English comprehension and he leaves me alone. It's Psycho Jordan I fear, hanging round the gates with his mates after school, taunting me.

'See you in the gym tomorrow, Overfeld. Better take out medical assurance!'

I long to turn and say, 'It's *in*surance, you dunce!' but I'm too scared, and I'm scared all the way home and half the night. I say to myself, *He can't hurt you in the gym with* *half the school watching.* But it's after the game I'm worried about. Who knows what he's capable of? He has that look which says, *I'm gonna bite your eyes out and boil 'em!*

seven

Next morning Mr Marvin has us for Geography and seems to have recovered.

'Enjoy the match yesterday, sir?' ventures Joey.

'What match?'

'Wasted by the Girlywimps, sir,' Lee Jordan reminds him.

Uproar! *Girlywimps, indeed!* Zulfi fuming, Tessa and Heather on their feet hurling abuse.

'*Silence!* Control yourselves. What do you think this is, the House of Commons? Thank you! That's more like it. Actually, it wasn't a bad game.'

Joey and his cronies can only laugh.

'Jeer all you like,' says Sir, 'but for a team with no stars and no experience, I thought they conducted themselves rather well, the girls included.'

'Thank you, sir!' Tessa says, and Zulfi hops up and bows to the class.

'Sit down, Malik. You might not be so cocky after this lot's finished with you.'

'Five–nil, sir,' Joey promises.

'Ten!' cries Winston.

'And a heap of bones,' murmurs Lee Jordan, who I'm thinking would have made a shining team-leader in the Hitler Youth.

In the gym at lunch-time, while Joey mingles with the audience taking bets on how heavily they're going to beat us, Zulfi gathers us together and tries to lift morale.

'We can do it,' he insists. 'Just mark tight and tackle hard and stay cool, and—'

'Oh shut up,' says Heather. 'Those snotty little windbags are gonna run rings round us. We were better off losing yesterday.'

'She's right,' says Tessa miserably. 'This is going to be seriously embarrassing.'

'We were brilliant yesterday,' wails Zulfi.

'Yeah, against a team even worse than us.'

'Maybe someone else should go in goal,' offers Oscar.

'Someone who can see,' Heather agrees.

'I don't believe this!' exclaims Zulfi.

'We're only being realistic.'

'I don't want *realistic*. I want you to believe we can win.'

'You're a hopeless dreamer, Zulf,' says Heather.

'I'd rather be a dreamer than a loser.'

'We'll never be able to show our faces again,' Tessa groans.

Zulfi pales. He's hurt, confused. I'm afraid he's going to burst into tears.

'If I might s-say something—' I pipe up.

'Yesterday was a laugh,' Tess's saying, 'but it's Joey's lot today, for God's sake.'

'All I'll be doing,' predicts Oscar gloomily, 'is picking the ball out of my net.'

'If you can find it,' laughs Heather.

'Please, please!' groans Zulfi. 'Don't do this to me.'

'All you can think about's yourself,' says Tess, 'but we're going to have to walk round school after this.'

'OK, fine!' Zulfi sees red. 'Do what you want, go ponce yourselves up and smoke ciggies in the jacks and practise your flaming cello and leave me and Sparky to take on the All Stars – and if Sparky wants to stick to his bottle-tops, that's fine too. I'll take them on alone, because I'd rather be a dreamer than a load of custard chickens going round saying *Ooh ooh, I don't wanna play cos of me image, ooh ooh ooh!* OK, fine! Push off then, all of you, go paint your nails!'

This has everyone flummoxed, and while we hesitate, I leap in again, 'If I might just s-s-say something . . .'

'*What*, Lewis?' snaps normally nice Tess.

Her anger throws me. Now *I* feel like bursting into tears.

'I just w-wanted to say I don't think they're all that g-good, and also, n-no matter what, we should try and stay n-nice to each other.'

They gaze at me. Encouraged, I stumble on, 'That's why they're so l-low in the l-league. They *think* they're g-good, and they're good at getting others to th-think they're g-good, but actually they're quite p-pedestrian.'

Quite *what*?

'Know something?' exclaims Tessa. 'He's right! They're rubbish.'

'Or r-rather,' I add excitedly, 'they're not *that* good and we're not *that* b-bad, and anyway, like Zulf said, it's not just about the w-w-w—'

'Yes!' Zulfi recalls. 'It doesn't matter what we lose by. Anyone can ponce round looking cool, but it takes guts to . . . to . . . to—' Snapping his fingers for the right words.

'To p-put yourself on the line,' I suggest.

'Right! You want respect, you got to put yourself on the line, face the fire, leap the flames—'

'OK, Zulf,' says Heather.

'March head high into the lion's den.'

'We get the message.'

'They're right,' says Tess. 'Worse thing we can do is back out and have everyone say we're scared.'

But when the moment comes, it *is* blood-stoppingly scary stepping into the gym to face the All Stars, the crowd pressing round the walls and filling the gallery, the opposition looking frighteningly cool, parading with all the swagger of veterans: Joey *the King* Spinx, stern-eyed and steady as he limbers up; *Calypso* Winston, smooth and dark and poised to burst out of his blocks; greased-back *Slicker* Lunn looking meaner than ever; Matthew *the Eagle* Fallon flexing his goalkeeper's shoulders, and *Psycho* Jordan swaying lightly side to side, staring at me and Zulfi in turn, a Doberman eyeing up a couple of whelps and licking his lips.

'Don't worry about him,' Zulfi whispers. 'He's all show.'

'Oh good,' I reply, 'that's a relief.'

I'm twitching uncontrollably, scared not just of Jordan but of freezing when the whistle goes. *You shone yesterday*, I tell myself.

But that other voice won't leave me alone. *That was wimp's luck, Lewis, you're going to mess up horribly today – so why not crawl back into your shell?*

Something's happening! Sir's pointing at Heather.

'I thought I sent you off yesterday.'

'So?'

'Well you're off then.'

'That was yesterday, sir,' Zulfi protests.

'Yes, and it earned a one-match suspension.'

'Thank God for that,' says Heather. 'Can I go now?'

'No!' says Tessa.

'I've things to do.'

'You're going nowhere, girl.' Seizing her friend's arm.

'She's not playing,' Sir repeats.

'*But sir*, this is schoolboy five-a-side,' Zulfi argues, 'not the flaming Premier League.'

'Don't *but sir* me, Malik. Football is football, and red is red.'

'School*boy* five-a-side?' Tessa objects, 'shouldn't that be school*person* five-a-side?'

'Or school*player* five-a-side,' Oscar reflects.

'Not that again.' Sir rolls his eyes. 'Off!' he orders Heather. 'Off!'

'I'm going, don't worry.'

'No!' Tessa yanks her back again. 'We can't play with four.'

'Whingers!' cry the All Stars. 'Whingers!'

'Let her play, sir, let 'em play with ten,' brags Joey. 'Won't make any difference.'

'Oh shuddup!' yells Heather.

The audience cheer, chaos threatens. 'Any more,' Sir warns, 'and I'll cancel the whole thing. Now, Malik, Heather is suspended, do you understand? Excluded, banned, *banished*.'

'But sir—'

'Sidelined, sin-binned, given the heave-ho, *comprendo*?'

'But sir—'

'Relieved of her post and altogether dispensed with – do I make myself clear?'

'Right then, I'm not playing.'

'What?'

'Not playing, sir.'

'Don't be ridiculous.'

'My team's coming off – come on.' Zulfi signals us to follow.

'Wait a minute, keep your hat on, Malik.' Sir rubs his tired eyes and sighs. 'For the tournament's sake and all the money we're raising, I'm going to be incredibly generous and give you sixty seconds to find a substitute player.'

Hands shoot up in the audience, offering to take Heather's place, but Zulfi's shaking his head. 'No Heather, no match.'

Zulfi can be quite dignified, never more than now, standing his ground, arms folded, reciting his mantra, 'No Heather, no match.'

'That's daft!' Joey pushes in.

'Tell him, sir,' cries Winston.

'Send him off too,' demands Lee Jordan.

Sir waves them away. 'Malik, pick a player, and be quick about it.'

'No Heather, no match.'

'Malik, do as I say!'

Scared but firm, 'No Heather, no match.'

'Malik, are you defying me?'

'Sorry, sir, but she's in, or we're out.'

Sir looks up to the heavens and screws up his face in exasperation. 'Who will rid me of this turbulent pupil?'

'Pleasure, sir,' says Heather, closing her fingers around Zulfi's scrawny neck.

Zulfi yelps, the gym shakes with laughter. This tournament is worth every penny.

Sir's flustered for once, unsure what to do – until Miss Scott comes to the rescue, drawing him aside for a quiet word, while all the time I'm thinking, Please, *please* call the match off so I don't make a monkey of myself!

Heather says, 'To hell with this, I'm off.'

'You crazy?' Zulfi says. 'You're an Invincible, you can't walk out.'

'Watch me!'

'Without you we've no defence,' he screeches. 'A ship with no mast, a rhino with no horn, a jugger with no barbs . . .'

'Leave me alone, I don't want to play!'

'You sure, Heather?' Tessa calls after her, pointing to the board, where *Invincibles* has been scratched out *again* and replaced with the dreaded *Girlywimps*.

Heather turns, squints, claps her hands on her hips and glares. 'Right, that's it!'

Sir shuffles over scratching his head. 'Somehow Miss Scott has persuaded me that it's in the interests of the tournament, disabled children everywhere and world peace that Jones plays.'

Zulfi lets out a delirious *'Yes!'* as if he just scooped Paulo Maldini from Milan.

My heart plunges; there's no way out. Any moment now the whistle will go and I'll be at the mercy of my terrors.

Mr Marvin calls the captains together and produces a coin.

Zulfi calls, 'Heads, sir – no! Tails – no!—'

'Malik!'

'Oh go on then, sir. Heads – or maybe—'

Too late. The coin spins, Zulfi loses, and *King* Joey steps up to kick off. He can't wait. It's in his eyes and the eyes of his teammates – they're going to make burgers out of us, thick with tomato ketchup. We take up our positions. Lee Jordan's cold dull eyes follow me, my heart wobbles. I'm a fraud, a pipsqueak, a wimp in a team of warriors. I so want to do well, but that voice keeps after me; *Who are you fooling, Lewis? get back to your logarithms* . . .

The whistle's gone, everything's in motion. Where's the ball? What am I doing? *Come on, Lewis!* I urge myself. *You'll never forgive yourself.*

As predicted, the game's not pretty. But nor is it one-sided. Thanks to whoever chalked Girlywimps on the board, our blood is up, and after the first anxious moments when the game scatters and early shots whistle past Oscar's head, we hurl ourselves into the fray.

'Sir, did you see that?' Joey complains.

'Get up, Spinx, you big teddy.'

'Oi sir, that was a foul.'

'Stop bleating, Daley, and get on with it.'

Mr Marvin might be expected to favour his All Stars, but if anything he's kinder to us as Zulfi, Tessa and a surprisingly mobile Heather pitch in with biting tackles, and Oscar, who seems to have caught the spirit of the moment, rushes off his line and throws himself recklessly at Winston's feet to save a certain score.

'Penalty, sir!' scream the All Stars. *'Penalty!'* But Sir waves play on, and, inspired by Oscar's bravery, I find myself thinking, *If Ozzy can do it* . . .

'Come on lads – and lasses of the revolution,' Zulfi urges us. 'Make 'em sweat!'

His words infect me, blood floods my brain, a passion I've never known possesses me, and after so many years mocked at school and squashed at home, something snaps in me – I'm an animal, relishing the fight, nipping at everybody's

83

heels. *Swines!* I'm thinking as I scrap with *Slicker* Lunn and tangle with *Calypso* Daley. *I'm sick of being pushed around – it's time I did a bit myself!*

'That's it, Sparky,' Zulfi calls. 'Stick it to them!'

We find ourselves in their half, pressurizing them, making *them* sweat for a change, forcing saves from Fallon, until when Sir blows for half-time, you can feel the change in the air. The All Stars are obviously going to win, but some of the swank's gone out of them.

The second half is just as manic. Joey's men come at us like lions, we harry them like hyenas, refusing to yield, questioning their superiority. And then an astonishing thing happens. Lee Jordan, running with the ball, doesn't spot me behind him, and as he ventures forward, weighing his options, I sneak the ball off him, look up, and slide-rule a pass to Zulfi who splits Lunn's legs with the spinning ball and unleashes a shot laced with months of misery – a shot so savage the ball carries Matthew Fallon into his own net.

GOAL!

'I saved it, sir, it never crossed the line,' Matthew bawls, but Sir saw it, everyone saw it, and Zulfi stands magnificent, saluting the crowd.

All Stars *NIL* – Invincibles *ONE*!

In all the excitement, my decisive contribution's barely noticed. But *I* noticed and I'm alight. My heart balloons. I'm carried away with happiness.

Time's running down, they come at us again and again, but they're starting to look ordinary, and we're beginning to look like Brazil, and you can tell the crowd's loving it, Joey's aristocrats humbled by Zulfi's oddballs.

But just when I'm thinking this is the best day of my life, and I'm picturing myself strolling round school to the tune of *brilliant, wicked, fantastic Sparky!*, everything turns sour. It happens so fast, Oscar fly-hacking the ball clear, the ball dropping towards me, and just as I go to trap it with someone closing on me from behind, I feel a sharp pain in the back of my thigh, an assault disguised as a tackle which Sir fails to see even as I drop in a groaning heap and Lee Jordan skips away innocent as a nun.

The rest of the game's a blur. I'm reduced to a hobbling crock as the All Stars press and press and force an equalizer. Our lungs fade, our legs die, Joey pots a simple winner and it's over. Heather sinks to her knees, Tessa drops her head, Zulfi's in tears and Oscar retrieves his specs and slinks away like a man released from a long jail term. I limp off in confusion, the crowd's applause in my ears.

In the showers, a relieved Joey mocks us anew, chanting, *Two-one, two-one, easiest win we ever won.'*

'Yeah and it was going to be ten, remember?' Zulfi scoffs. 'Or was it fifteen?'

'Invincibles indeed! With a decent ref it *would* have been fifteen.'

'Rubbish!' Zulfi is incensed. 'Sparky's right, you're nothing but a load of pedestrians!'

Joey's heroes fall silent and look at me. They're not impressed. Lee Jordan steps out of the shower, horribly naked, and nails me with his gaze. 'What did you call us?'

My heart thickens. I want to blurt out, *You don't frighten me*, but I'm scared, and so is Zulfi, I can tell. Just the two of us in here – Oscar's skipped off somewhere; cellists don't take showers – against five of them.

'I'm talking to you, you stuttering sparrow,' says Jordan. 'What do you mean, *pedestrians?*'

'Leave him alone,' says Zulfi. 'You're always picking on him.'

'What's the matter, can't he talk for himself?'

'Yes I c-c-can!' I reply, and trying to forget the shooting pain in my leg, I hang a towel round my bird-frame and stand straight, conscious of another big moment, bigger than anything in the gym, because this is *real*, realer than football, and the real test is, can I stand up to these bully boys? I'd like to report that this stuttering sparrow, refusing to be intimidated, looks Jordan in the eye and tells him to his face that he and his mates have all the foot-balling talent of a pile of planks, and that he's a coward, a thug and a stinking cheat – but in the Arctic glare of his gaze, all I can muster is, 'I s-simply s-said I don't think you lot are as g-good as you think.'

'Oh! Wow, listen to the expert!' Joey laughs.

'We weren't even trying!' jeers Jordan.

'Never got out of first gear,' Lunn agrees.

I'm trembling, but I'm not running.

'And I t-told Sir I thought Zulfi should be in the school t-team.'

'That crybaby,' laughs Joey.

'He's useless,' says Lee Jordan.

'Totally useless,' says *Slicker* Lunn, always in greasy agreement with Jordan.

'We made you sweat,' Zulfi hisses.

'Oh yeah!'

'Gave you the fright of your lives!'

'Oh sure!'

'Made you sweat and earned *respect*!'

'Yeah, but you still lost,' grins Winston.

'D-doesn't matter,' I hear myself cry, 'we deserved to win.'

They gaze at me in wonder. Then laugh even harder and come at us with wet towels, flicking viciously at our unprotected flesh, making us flinch and cry like startled hens.

eight

I'm hoping the limp loosens so no-one notices, but it feels like my leg's filled with hot cement. Every step is agony, and by the time I get home I can barely stand.

Mum's appalled. 'What happened?'

'Nothing m-much.'

'Nothing much? Look at you!'

'We were r-raising money for ch-ch-charity.'

'How on earth do you get injured raising money for charity?'

'Someone t-tackled me a bit hard.'

'Tackled? What do you mean *tackled*?'

'In the g-gym.'

'In the gym? What were you doing in the gym?'

'Playing in a t-tournament.'

'Tournament?'

'F-football.'

'*Football?*' she blurts, as though I just

confessed to fire-eating or high-wire juggling.

She makes me drop my trousers, gasps. 'Goodness, have you seen this?'

I'm just as horrified. The back of my thigh looks like it's been injected with ink and blown up with a bicycle pump. Lee Jordan must have swung his knee like a hammer. I could cheerfully kill him, and imagine a crash course in karate, an ugly confrontation in the jacks, a single blow that snaps his neck like a chicken. Mum applies lashings of ice which nearly makes me sick, and drives to the chemist for a very large bandage.

'I've never understood the appeal of football, but I have noticed your stammer getting worse.'

'Everybody plays f-football, Mum. It's n-normal.'

'You're not everybody, Lewis, and coming home with an elephant's leg isn't normal, and I'm quite determined to send you *twice* a week to speech therapy.' She looks at me exasperated. 'When are you going to wake up, Lewis? *I* never had your opportunities, I *walked* two miles to school and *shared* textbooks with a neighbour, *if* I was lucky. I was bright, but the school had no facilities and my mum couldn't afford private coaching, so I left school with nothing, *nothing*, you understand?'

'I know, Mum, you've t-told us.'

'Well, it obviously hasn't sunk in. Now what about your homework?'

It's hard to think past the pain. 'Um, we've to translate a p-page called Madame somebody-or-other's *Pharmacie*, and for Computer Studies read the ch-chapter on artificial intelligence – you know, like whether computers can ever hope to c-compete with humans when they've no f-feelings or anything – computers, that is, not—'

'Fine, is that it?'

'No, there's tomorrow's d-debate to prepare, the h-horse versus the c-car, pros and cons, like the one produces useful w-waste while the other belches nasty f-fumes, and also cars can't jump gates or c-cross rivers, whereas a f-farmer living in a remote area can rely on his h-horse to bring him h-home if he's drunk too much – the f-farmer that is, not the h-horse; while on the other hand—'

'Yes, dear, that's fine, now you get on to it while I do dinner, and if that leg's hurting, you'll just have to grin and bear it, *because* . . . ?' Eyebrows raised and a knowing smile . . .

'My w-work comes first.'

'Good boy.'

I hobble up to my room and take a peek at my bottle-tops; a few hurried flicks on the floor, Lewis Overfeld darting between Carlsberg and Stella Artois to fire past Guinness in the Roma goal! *Unbelievable!*

Rufus licks my hand, my sister kisses me goodnight, my mum gives me a pain-numbing tablet and turns out the light. I lie in a haze of disappointment. If only we'd beaten the All Stars I'd suffer my leg with a smile. But their taunts echo in my head, and worse, I failed the big test, I didn't stand up to the bullies, and to escape this painful thought, I lie awake reliving the moment I stole the ball from Jordan and set Zulfi up for that murderous goal.

The phone goes late, my father checking in from some godforsaken town after a show, Mum reporting that 'Lewis has been playing football' (horror of horrors) 'and he has the most appalling injury' (you'd think I'd suffered brain damage) 'and I want you to have a serious talk with him, because his mind's obviously not on his work, his stammer's getting worse by the minute and

I'm afraid his fascination with football will be the ruin of him.' (Like vodka, I suppose, or heroin.)

'Bruised, yes, that's what I said – no! No! Nothing broken, but you should see it, darling, it's *purple!* And bloated. It's absolutely appalling – I'm going to have to speak to Mr Marvin.'

Listening to this I feel shaky, my stomach a hive of nerves, and all at once I'm struck by a terrible thought – it's my mum I'm most afraid of: my mum who scares me to death, who treats me like a six-year-old and runs my life like a pedigree spaniel, or worse, a robot. She's got my whole life programmed. Apart from *Toast or cereals this morning?* or *What do you want for your birthday?* I haven't a say in anything. Even my birthday guest list is checked for undesirables, and I have to beg politely for Zulfi's inclusion because he's not *our sort* and doesn't *speak properly*. I want to tell her that speech therapy's no use – I can't breathe, that's the problem. I go to bed anxious and I wake up anxious and I'm anxious all day. Isn't that how you're supposed to get ill, being anxious all the time? I'm sick of being anxious. I love my mum but I'm scared of her.

The house is silent, everyone asleep, but I lie in the grip of the awful realization that the really *really* big challenge I'm going to have to face – bigger than shining in the gym, bigger than dealing with bullies – is right here, at home. I'm going to have to stand up to my mum.

It's roasting under the duvet, but I'm cold.

nine

Mum puts me in a taxi. The driver offers to drop me at the school door, but I'd rather die than be seen getting out of a cab so he leaves me in the lane and I hitch myself up and beg my leg to co-operate, because I don't want to walk in with a limp. But the thigh's stiff and the pain's sharp and when I walk it feels like a crocodile's clamped to my leg. I can't help it, I hobble into class where Mr Marvin cocks a crooked eyebrow.

'Took a bit of a knock did we, yesterday?'

'A vicious kick,' Zulfi corrects him.

'Really? And what have you to say, Lewis? Just Lewis, thank you, Malik, he has his own voice box.'

What a thrilling moment when I swivel in my seat and point dramatically at Lee Jordan and say, *Yes, sir, that vicious rat-faced, devil-eyed thug put me out of the game on purpose.*

If only! Instead I feel Jordan's eyes on the back of my neck and shrug like it wasn't that bad and who's complaining anyway?

Zulfi's most definitely complaining. 'You didn't even give a foul, sir.'

'I didn't give a foul, Malik, because I didn't see one.'

'Perfectly fair tackle, sir,' pronounces Joey.

'Rubbish, we was robbed!' says Zulfi.

'*Were* robbed, Malik.'

Zulfi, surprised, 'You admit it then, sir?'

'Load of whingers, sir,' says Jordan.

'Whingers, sir,' echoes *Slicker* Lunn.

'*Bulltwist!*' Zulfi cries.

'Malik, how dare you use a word like that in class!'

'But sir, I only said—'

'I know what you only said.'

'I didn't say—'

'I know what you didn't say. See me after school. And you, Overfeld.'

Me – why me?

The rest of the day is a bellyful of nerves and anxiety, made worse by our enemies.

'You two are in *big* trouble!'

'Questioning sir's reffing and using foul language.'

'Malik will be suspended – *if* he's lucky.'

'Expelled more like.'

'And Flusher made to clean out the loos!'

'And crucified – for Caesar's birthday!'

Hoots of laughter.

'Leave us alone!' snaps Zulfi. Our tormentors wander off laughing. Zulfi's depressed. 'I've blown it, my football career's finished. I've as much chance of making the team as winning the Noble Peace Prize.'

'I th-think that should be No-*bel* Prize, Zulf.'

'Just when I thought we proved ourselves. Why can't I keep my big mouth shut?'

I'm depressed too. 'It wouldn't feel so bad if I'd managed to s-stand up to Jordan in the sh-showers yesterday.'

'You *did* stand up to him.'

'I *did*?'

'Sure you did. You told him they weren't all that good.'

'Yes but I didn't tell Jordan what a b-bully, c-coward and a ch-cheat he is.'

'Well you *half* stood up to him. That's a start.'

'Yes, I suppose so,' I murmur gratefully.

After school we stand like two puppets facing Mr Marvin.

'Stand straight, the pair of you. You're a disgrace, Overfeld, what are you?'

'A disgrace, sir, but w-w-why?'

'If Jordan deliberately injured you, have the guts to say so. And as for you, Malik, what was that word you polluted the air with earlier?'

'What, *robbed*, sir?'

Mr Marvin blinks, unsure whether Zulfi's being witty or dim. 'I want one hundred lines; *I must not use bad language in class.*'

'Ah, *sir.*'

'Never mind *ah sir.*'

'But honest, sir, don't you think we *was* robbed.'

'No! I think you *were* robbed. Dear, God, why do I waste my time?'

'So you *do* think we was robbed?'

'*Yes*, Malik!' Rolling his eyes. 'Robbed blind – a complete travesty.'

'Complete what, sir?'

'An injustice, an inequity, a wholly un-merited result! You were a revelation, the pair of you.'

'A what, sir?'

'Not so much stick insect as *scorpion*, and rather more *sparrowhawk* than sparrow. And you two displayed a precious quality my established strikers appear to lack, namely . . .' leaning back thoughtfully in his chair, hands behind his head, 'a natural rapport.'

'Natural what, sir?'

'Lewis seemed always to know where you were – the sparrowhawk feeding the scorpion – and I confess, gentlemen,' sitting up and contemplating us sternly, as if it were somehow our fault, 'you've got me thinking.'

'In what way, sir?'

'Spinx and Daley have their moments, but they've no rapport.'

'And we're loaded with rapport, aren't we, sir.'

'They keep missing each other.'

'They'd miss each other in the same pair of boots, sir!'

'Three matches to go and we're perilously near the foot of the table.'

'Can't have that, sir,' Zulfi tut-tuts sadly. 'Poor Miss Proudfoot, you've got to *do* something.'

'Thank you for your advice, Zulfi. It's just such a pity you chose to use such bad language earlier.'

Zulfi and I exchange looks. 'Ah sir, you wouldn't want to hold that against us,

not when you're looking at the great-
est striking partnership since Owen
and Shearer, since Figo and Gomez, since
Youri Djorkaeff and Thierry Henry,
since—'

'Thank you, Zulfi.'

'Malik and Overfeld leading the line –
sounds good, eh, sir?'

'*Thank you!*'

Mr Marvin's praise sets my blood racing.
I'm dizzy with happy nerves. I may be
limping, but my heart skips all the way
home. I'm not a meek little sparrow after
all. I've claws and a mean beak and wings
that throw shadows.

I check my new identity in the diction-
ary. My eyes are tired and I look up the
wrong word and discover that I'm a small
headless wedge-shaped nail used for
mending shoes. *What?* Can't be! Oh, thank
goodness, I'm looking at Sparrow*bill*.
Underneath I find Sparrow*hawk*, which
says I'm a small hawk of the genus
Accipiter preying on small birds and
mammals. I'm a predator!

But I'm an injured predator, and an
anxious one. Sir wants us to begin training
with the team, but it could take days, *weeks*

for my leg to recover. And Sir's told the others about us and some aren't happy. The looks Joey and Jordan give us make my blood freeze.

Sir says to soak the leg in hot water and then in cold and then hot again, and gently stretch it and rest it, and think positive thoughts to help it heal. But do I really want to heal and have to confess to Mum that I may be playing for the school? Do Zulfi and I really want to face the fury of our tormentors?

In the damp windblown playground we seek the warmth of friends.

'Sparrow and Skinny playing for the school team!' Tessa saunters over to congratulate us.

'Great stuff, Sparkplug!' Heather claps me on the back, nearly knocking me over.

'We're not playing yet, man,' Zulf explains. 'There's no promises.'

'And I won't be p-playing anyway,' I say casually.

''Course you will,' Tessa throws an arm round my shoulders and I nearly pass out with excitement. 'You were great. Not as good as me, but pretty good – for a sparrow.'

'It's no good, guys, c-count me out.'

'*Why?*'

'I've t-tons of work to do.'

'Don't be daft!'

'No law says swots can't score goals,' says Heather grandly.

'He's scared of Joey and Lee Jordan,' Zulfi guesses.

'*What?*' Tessa twists her nose in scorn. 'Are you going to let those yobs spoil your dream?'

'Scumbags,' says Heather. 'You don't wanna worry about them.'

The girls leave us. Zulfi says, 'You've come this far, you can't duck out now. Without you, man, I'm on me tod, lonely as baloney, Laurel without Hardy, Butch without Cassidy, Marks without Spencer – are you listening, man?'

I am, but I'm still dazed by the sensation of Tessa's arm round my shoulders. 'I'm l-listening.'

'Forget Joey and those bums. Concentrate on getting fit and dazzling Sir with our *rapport*.'

I'm smiling sadly. 'OK, f-forget the bully boys but what about my m-mum?'

'Listen, man, you're going to have to cook up some serious white lies.'

'I don't w-want to tell lies all my l-life. At

some point, I've got to s-stand up for myself.'

Zulfi examines me closely. 'You serious?'

I frown – *sort of.*

Shaking his head doubtfully. 'I can't see it, Winnie the Pooh taking on *Jaws*!'

'My m-mum's not that bad.'

'Mickey Mouse tangling with Mike Tyson.'

'Very f-funny.'

Zulfi shrugs. It's all right for him; his mum's so busy making ends meet she hasn't time to worry about him.

My dad's coming home Sunday. Mum says he wants to talk to me.

'W-what about?' I ask innocently.

'About your work, darling, your future.'

What am I to do? Sit there while Dad lectures me and not say a word? I can't do that any more. I'm ten months short of thirteen, for goodness' sake.

This is it – I sense – *the crunch is coming.*

My leg's loosening all the time. Soon I'll be ready to take my chance in the school team. Mum knows nothing about it, only that my school marks have been slipping recently. I'm doing my best but I can't concentrate. I'm trying to let her see I'm working hard, reading more than I need, writing more than expected, putting thought into essays and projects, but all the time I'm waiting and watching for the right moment to tackle her, wondering how I'll recognize it when it comes, and will I have the courage to go through with it?

It's tough being a wimp.

Meanwhile I stand on a frosty touchline watching Zulfi train with the team. He's having a rough time. Joey and Winston resent him and they won't pass to him, pretending they haven't noticed him screaming for the ball. And Lee Jordan can't stand him and gets in all the nasty tackles he can. But I needn't worry. Once Zulfi sets his mind on something, nothing will move him. The look in his eyes says, *You're not getting rid of me.* He's like a dog with his teeth in a burglar's bum.

He hobbles off afterwards, bony legs marked by Jordan's boots, but he's not complaining. He's in among them now.

The wink he gives me says, *Are they sweating, or what!*

Saturday arrives. My leg's OK and I'd like to report that Zulfi and I are on the pitch leading the line against modest Oakthorpe, but the truth is we're freezing our bums on the subs' bench – the subs' plastic milkcrate actually – waiting patiently for Sir's call. *Im*patiently in Zulfi's case, because Winston and Joey manage to get in each other's way and still score the only goal of the game. A circus of leaps and hoots greets the final whistle. You'd think Saley Marsh Middle School had just routed Real Madrid.

'Didn't we do brill, sir?' brags Joey.

'Wasted 'em, didn't we, sir?' laughs Winston.

Sir's not impressed. 'Play like that next Saturday and you'll be the ones that's wasted.'

'*Who are*, s-sir,' I correct him cheerfully.

'*What*, Lewis?'

'*Who are* w-wasted, sir . . . not *that's wasted.*'

'Thank you, Lewis, most helpful.'

'Sir.' Zulfi tugging his sleeve.

'What is it now?'

'I thought you were going to play us?'

'The way they played today, you never know.'

'But when, sir? There's only two games left.'

'Malik,' Sir reproaches him, 'you don't ask questions like that.'

'But think about poor Miss Proudfoot, sir, all that school tradition. Saley Marsh needs strikers with good looks, speed and rapport.'

'Thank you for your advice, Malik, I shall bear it in mind.'

In class, Sir gazes out the window. Miss Proudfoot has been in to express satisfaction with Saturday's win, but her praise is as warm as a pail of ice and Mr Marvin's left in no doubt that she expects us to repeat the feat against Broadstones and Pemberton Hall.

He keeps looking over at me and Zulfi, wondering – wondering, *Shall I stick with my established but uninspired strikers – or take a risk with the Sparrowhawk and the Scorpion?*

At lunch he's seen deep in conversation with Mrs Okocha. She's making some peculiar proposal, spreading her hands as if to say, *What have you to lose?* Sir frowns doubtfully, but whatever it is, he's intrigued.

Later, Zulfi tracks me to the library, giddy with the news that Mrs Okocha has some unusual contacts and is arranging a friendly match against surprising opposition.

'Mr Marvin's agreed and he's putting us on trial.'

'Don't you mean g-giving us a trial?'

'Joey and Winston will have the first half – you and me the second.'

'Against who?'

'A weird foreign team called God Is For Referees or something.'

'*God is for Referees?* Are you s-sure?'

'Our big chance, Sparrow!'

'*Shhh*, k-keep it down, this is a l-library.'

'I only hope it's serious opposition – they sound like a bunch of nerds – but everybody's talking about it. This is it, man, we're in business!'

'Wait a s-sec. God is for Referees? *Godisfor* . . . You sure that isn't Kosovar? You sure r-referees isn't *refugees*. You know, from the w-war?'

'What war?'

'Where Nato b-bombed the Serbs out of K-Kosovo . . .'

Zulfi has no interest in the wider world; getting by day to day is plenty. Me, I love the news: wars, earthquakes, aborigines demanding their rights, dictators getting their comeuppance and pets rescuing their owners from rivers.

'Wow, Zulf, if they are K-Kosovans – we could be part of living h-history!'

Zulfi's looking puzzled. 'Won't be much of a match.'

'Why?'

'Aren't refugees all old and sick?'

'Not n-necessarily. They're people who flee their country cos of war or p-persecution.'

'Oh, OK.'

'Anyone can be a r-refugee. You're a bit of a refugee, Zulfi, and so am I. So is everyone who doesn't feel he b-belongs.'

'But won't they be tired?'

'I shouldn't think so. All that running for cover, they might be quite quick.'

ten

I've yet another parental consent form in my pocket – Tuesday after school, Saley Marsh Middle School versus some unpronounceable team from Kosovo. Somebody has to sign it and I doubt they'll accept Lindsay's carefully joined-up script or Rufus's pawprint.

No signature, no play.

My father's home, with flowers for Mum, the new Harry Potter for Lindsay and a smart pencil and biro set for me. Rufus goes potty and pees on the floor, Lindsay jumps into her daddy's arms and I get my head ruffled as usual. He smiles at me a lot, uneasy I suppose, because he's away so much and knows we don't like it, and now he's got to talk to me and it's not his sort of thing. My dad loves us in his way but gets fidgety at home. Walking Rufus, collecting

Lindsay from dance class, testing me on French verbs, watching TV with Mum and the odd dinner party – a few weeks of that and he's away like a dog off the lead.

It's Sunday. Mum takes Lindsay shopping, leaving me and Dad *alone*. Dad rummages about for his cigarettes, running fingers through his hair, desperate for a smoke. Between them, Mum and Dad make our airy home smell like a rubbish tip. They're worriers, my parents, nervous wrecks. I can see where I get it from. Look at Dad now, pacing up and down sucking on poison.

'Can we go to the p-park – knock a b-ball about?'

'Bit chilly isn't it, Lewy?'

'We'll soon w-warm up.'

'What about your leg?'

'It's f-fine now. And guess what . . .'

'What?'

I want to tell him I've been selected – yes me, harmless Lewis – to represent the school in a friendly match and I've got the consent form upstairs.

'I need the p-practice.'

He's looking at me, but he's not listening.

'D-Dad, I've another f-form for you to s-sign . . .'

'What? Not now, Lewis . . . look, sit down a minute, will you.'

I sit on the sofa, open space either side of me, Dad in his armchair tapping his fingers, me uncomfortable in my skin, twiddling my toes.

'Your mother's worried about you, Lewy.'

I'm not scared really, just sad. My father doesn't mean any of this. What the critics say about his performances, that's what excites him, not my school reports.

'I said your mum's worried about you, Lewy . . .'

I want to say to him, Mum worries about *everything*.

'She's concerned that, well, you're letting things distract you from your work.'

He waits for me to respond, but I hate it when he's like this and I say nothing. At least Mum believes in her rules.

'By *things*, she means your current infatuation with football and, to be frank, some of the company you're keeping . . . chap called Zulfi, I think, who your mother doesn't deem ideal friendship material.'

He conjures up a sympathetic smile. 'Look, mate, I do understand. I was like you once, wrong sort of friends and new distractions which seemed deeply important at the time – in my case music, as you know. I so wanted to be in a band! . . . But your mother's right, it can all come later. Right now you've got to knuckle down and get the grades. No good coming home with a leg the size of a tree trunk. Bottle-tops are terrific, but not the real thing, you're not cut out for it. So why not forget about football *and* drama and find yourself a friend you've more in common with, someone with *ambition*!'

I return his gaze, thinking, you don't make friends that way, you don't pick them like a pair of shoes. You just like someone, and they like you, and neither of you really knows why. You just feel comfy together, you trust each other. I'm not going to dump Zulfi and go shopping for a better brand of friend.

My eyes prick at the thought of losing Zulfi and having no-one.

'I know it's tough, Lewy, but your mum knows what's best for you.' He gives a happy little laugh; he's done his duty and now he'll probably pat me on the knee and fetch a beer and suggest we see if there's a film on telly.

But before he can move I have a question. 'Dad?'

'Yes?'

'Did you let your f-funny friends and m-music interfere with *y-your* work?'

'God, yes, never did a thing, shocking grades, you should have seen them.'

'Well, you see *I* don't.'

'Pardon?'

'Let anything interfere with my w-work. I work h-hard and my t-teachers are pleased with me.'

In other words, *so there!*

Dad blinks. 'Won't be a sec,' he says and goes looking for a beer.

Sorry, Dad – I feel like saying – *you don't understand and you never were like me.*

'Shall we see what's on the box?' he calls.

'No thanks, I've w-work to do.'

Mum comes to kiss me goodnight, looks at me for signs that *the talk* went well.

'Everything all right, dear?'

The consent form lies inches from her hand, folded in the pages of *Great Expectations*. She's got to sign it right now, or latest tomorrow evening. The moment passes, her lips brush my cheek, she switches out the light.

Standing up to Dad, in my own small way, is all I can manage for one day.

eleven

Monday drags fearfully. They're all talking and fretting about the Kosovo game.

'Relax, gentlemen,' Sir reassures us. 'We're not parachuting into the former Yugoslavia, we won't be dodging bombs or ducking missiles. It's a thirty-minute drive to a field on the outskirts of Ravenscar for heaven's sake.'

'But sir, my dad says we're only twelve and shouldn't be playing grown-ups.'

'Who said anything about grown-ups?'

'But you said refugees, sir.'

'Yes, Mr Fallon, because strange as it may seem, refugees do sometimes have children. Do you really think I'd let you play a team of grown men?'

After our dismal showing in yesterday's spelling test, actually *yes!*

'You're playing a *junior* team, *sons* of refugees – dear oh dear!'

My stomach crawls. What am I to do?

Mum will go mad. She'll say, 'I don't believe it! Your father has just explained our feelings and you have the gall to ask me to sign this?' I'm even quieter than usual and Sir notices.

'Looking forward to your big day, Lewis?'

'Very m-much, sir.' I smile widely, pleased as Punch, sick as a sausage.

'You OK, Sparrow?' Heather slaps me on the back at lunch. 'You look like you seen a ghost.'

I have, I'm thinking – my own.

'What's up, Sparks?' Tessa hangs her arm around me again and I can feel my knees going, 'Stop worrying. You two are going to be *invincible*! Can't wait to see Joey and Winston's faces.'

Alone with Zulfi I let the mask drop.

'Man, what's wrong?'

I can hardly breathe. 'It's n-no use. I c-can't do it, Zulf.'

'*What?* What are you talking about? We been through this, we're great together, Dennis and Gnasher, Jekyll and Hyde, Zulf-the-Wolf and Supersparrow! We'll have those refugees for tea!'

'Thanks, Zulfi, but—'

'We'll be unbelievable, man. Like Sir said, we're telepathetic!'

'Telepathic, I think, Zulf.'

'Wherever I go you'll feed me, right?'

'Y-you don't understand. That form, Zulf . . . the consent form . . .'

He stares at me. The penny drops like a rock. *'Blast!* Your mum. I forgot. Won't your dad sign it?'

'No, he's a yes-dear, no-dear, anything-you-say-dear sort of d-dad.'

Zulfi's thinking. If anybody can get me out of this . . .

'I got it. Fake a letter saying you're going on a geography field trip.'

'A letter would have to l-look authentic.'

'What?'

'Real.'

'On your computer!'

'Out of the blue, a f-field trip? She'd never f-fall for that.'

'Man, you gotta take chances, you gotta be brave, you got to lie sometimes.'

'I don't like l-lying.'

'Then stick to flipping bottle-tops and stop wasting my time.'

I look at him. He looks at me.

'Sorry, Sparrow, didn't mean that.' We walk on. He's thinking hard. Stops. 'Got it! You don't need to fake anything.'

'I don't.'

'Sign it yourself.'

'*What!*'

'She'll never know.'

'And how will I exp-p-p . . . ?'

'Explain what?'

'Coming home l-late?'

'I got that too. You're doing some revising at someone's house – *my* house. She'll love that. You and me swotting for a test.'

We hurry on to the bus stop, Zulfi chuffed with himself, me wondering how to tell him my mum wouldn't want me revising anywhere near him? The bus crawls in the traffic, Zulfi rabbiting on about tomorrow's match, me squirming inside, and now he's laughing.

'What's f-funny?'

'Your face, Sparrow. You're faking her signature, not raiding her bank account.'

'It's not j-just that.'

'I know, she doesn't like me.'

'How do you know?'

'That time you brought me home, I could see she hated me.'

'No! You're wrong. She fixed us a big tea, she was r-really nice to you.'

'Yeah, real polite and real cold. I felt as welcome as a bad smell.'

'I'm s-sorry, Zulf, I didn't know.'

117

'You could be revising with – let me see – Oscar. No! Tess, she's nearer, she'll do it.'

'Think so?'

'Course, relax, it's cool.'

We've reached Zulfi's stop. He's getting off.

'H-how will I know everything's OK?'

'I'll phone.' He skips down the stairs. 'Two rings and I'll hang up and you'll know it's sorted.'

Lucky Zulfi living two streets from Tess. They bump into each other sometimes. I wish I *was* working at her place tomorrow instead of playing in a match where I'm bound to mess up. I wish I hadn't got into this.

But it's too late to back out. I'm walking home with the form in my pocket itching to be signed. Rufus leaps to lick me, my mother takes my coat and asks me to help Lindsay with her sums before doing my homework. I'm sick with worry, trying to remember what Mum's signature looks like. Her handwriting's bold and passionate. She wanted to be an artist when she was young and you can easily imagine her attacking canvases in a paint-spattered studio. But where will

I find an example of her signature?

'Lewis,' Lindsay pinches me. 'Concentrate!'

'*Ouch!*'

'You're supposed to be helping me.'

'I am, I am.'

My sister's not like me. She's only eight, but she's a sturdy little devil, funny and fearless. She's not afraid of Mum – they fight like cats – but *I am*, and the thought of borrowing one of her credit cards to forge her signature makes me want to throw up.

The phone goes. I prick my ears; it rings once, twice and stops before anyone can reach it. So Zulfi's spoken to Tessa, and she's said, *No sweat, I'll say he's with me.* She's a great girl, though I hate the way she goes on about Matthew Fallon and I want to tell her, *But Tess, he may be tall and have nice wavy hair but he has the brains of an ox and no personality!*

'Lewis, *concentrate*!'

'*Ouch*, that hurt!'

'You're dreaming.'

'I'm sorry, but I have to do s-something. I'll be right back.'

I don't stammer much with Lindsay – nor with Zulf. I don't know why, whereas now, standing at the top of the stairs like someone ready to leap from a bridge, I go cold and I feel my stammer rising like something from the deep.

'M-Mum . . . ?' I find her at the dining table, writing reports.

'I'm busy dear, what is it?'

'I'm invited round to Tessa H-Hacket's h-house after school tomorrow to go through our p-projects – if that's OK? I could be l-late. I mean I *will* be late – if that's O-OK?'

She peers at me over her specs. 'Who's Tessa Hacket?'

'She's in my c-class. She's very c-clever.'

'You've never mentioned her.'

Panic. 'Her father's a c-composer . . .'

'Really?' Mum sounds impressed. Actually her dad's unemployed and sings in pubs but he does perform some of his own compositions.

'And her m-mum's h-high up in the post office . . .'

Actually her mum works behind the counter in the post office but it is high up on Dippling Rise.

'Well, I don't see why not. Sounds a good idea. We'll discuss it later.'

I'm shocked at myself, such wicked lies. And the deception gets worse as I find

120

excuses to wander through the house – *I need a glass of water . . . I must have dropped my pencil-sharpener somewhere* – trying to locate my mother's handbag. I even drop my pencil-sharpener on purpose and sidefoot it under an armchair so I can *find* it if necessary. But the handbag's not in the kitchen, the living room or dining area. It's not in the entrance hall where she sometimes leaves it. It must be in her bedroom, which is a bummer because what possible reason would I have to be in there? I stagger on with my homework but can't focus. I'll have to tell Sir I was unwell, another lie. I can't bear it. Why can't I have normal parents who sign forms without even looking up from the TV?

I can hear Mum on the phone below, a chance to leave my desk, slip into her room and cast about. No bag in sight, but it could be under the dressing-table or behind the bed if I venture further. I turn, listen – she's still on the phone – tiptoe deeper into the room. No handbag – *blast!* Do I dare press on . . . into her lemony bathroom with its angled mirrors and forests of lotions, a private place where she doesn't like us going? Could she have left it in here when soaking her lenses? If she catches me I've had it, because Lindsay and I have our own small bathroom, so why would I be in here?

What's that? Footsteps on the stairs? She's coming up! Oh God, she *is* up! She's coming in. I'm trapped. What will I say? – *Oh hi, Mum, this seems to be your bathroom, how silly of me!*

She's in the bedroom, opening a wardrobe, hanging something up or taking it out, leaving me to cast about for somewhere to hide. But where in this narrow little – *there!* The only possible place, the ceiling-high cupboard, the one Mum hates anyone – even Trudi the cleaner – disturbing, and I'm inching towards it, trying desperately not to make a sound, prising open the double doors with quivering fingers and gazing at half a dozen shelves packed with bathrobes and towels, packs of loo paper, Kleenex, stacks of shampoo, a store sufficient to see off a medieval siege. I opt for the bottom level where there seems to be space inside the arsenal of disinfectants.

Crawling in and crouching down without a sound is hard enough, but closing the doors from inside is *impossible*! I can pull one door shut, but the other comes only so far and traps my fingers, and now – *what's that?* Squeaking floorboards, footsteps over the carpet. She's coming, humming crossly to herself as she enters, her feet visible through the gap in the doors as she crosses to the loo.

I shut my eyes tight and cover my ears. My squashed body hurts, my thoughts scatter. What am I doing? How did I get into this? Who cares about a game of flaming football? The loo's flushing, unseen water thunders by, I can hear the rustle of clothes, a tap running, the clank of the towel ring against the wall, and then – *nothing*. I open my eyes and realize by the angle of her feet that my mother's peering at the cupboard, wondering why it's open. Her own childhood was overshadowed by poverty and she's a hoarder, a snapper-up of bargains. No-one comes in here without permission. *Oh no*, she's coming, flinging the doors wide! I screw up my eyes and brace myself, hear her breathing as she checks her precious store. She must see me – she *must!*

The doors close. She's gone. I'm in the dark, heart drumming. I'll wait a bit. Then I'll crawl out and try and get back to my room. I'm an agent on his first mission behind enemy lines. I got in all right, but can I get out?

Later, watching TV with Lindsay, marvelling at my narrow escape and wondering where on earth Mum's put her handbag, she enters the room *holding it*, looks me in the eye and says, 'Is this what you're looking for?'

I return her gaze, speechless. Blood drains from my face.

'Rufus found it. Here.' She's holding out my pencil-sharpener.

Rufus is nudging me, wagging his tail and urging me to throw the sharpener so he can retrieve it.

'So you want to visit – Tessa, was it? – tomorrow. How far does she live?'

'Not f-far. They'll b-bring me home.'

'I'll want her address and phone number and I want you back by seven-thirty.'

'F-fine.' Except that I don't know Tessa's address or number. 'I'll have to ch-check tomorrow and c-call you.'

Mum smiles teasingly, 'Is she pretty – this Tessa?'

I'm going red. 'W-well, yes, actually.'

It's bedtime. Mum's left her handbag on the hall table, which come to think of it is where she generally leaves it at night. I read in bed, listening to her on the phone below; 'That's right, a classmate's house — *a girl!* — quite pretty he admits . . . her father's a composer, the mother in the higher echelons of the post office . . .'

I read on, same page over and over, trying to stay calm, trying not to think about the handbag downstairs, waiting for Mum to come in and say goodnight, and then I stay awake till she turns in, and wait for the radio she plays softly in the bath to stop, and then I wait for the house to fall quiet and then give it another half hour until midnight because I know she likes to read, and then *another* half hour before finally I dare creep to the door and look out. There's no light under her door, no sound from her room. The stairs are dimly lit by street light in the landing window. I pick my way past my sister's room on the left, mother's on the right, lifting one foot at a time, setting it gently down and wincing each time a loose board creaks. The stairs are worst, crying out, *Wake up Mrs Overfeld, your son's up to something!*

My excuse if she comes out? *Sorry, Mum, I was suddenly starving and fancied some bread and butter.*

Down, down and down, one treacherous

step at a time. If only I wasn't so scared I'd slide down the banisters. For the moment all's quiet above and below as I trip softly across the hall floor to where the handbag leans on the table like a Spanish galleon bloated with treasure, when suddenly *someone's there* – a silhouette in motion in the living room, rising from the sofa and coming for me! – and I turn the other way to call Rufus from his basket to save me when out the living room comes not some intruder to hit me over the head but Rufus himself, daring to sleep on the sofa. *Bad boy, you're lucky Mum didn't catch you!* He's jumping up to lick my face!

'Shhh . . .' I beg him. 'Shhh . . .' Smothering his chops.

A door above! Footfalls on the landing – *Mum!*

'Rufus, what is it? What's going on?'

I try to hold on to him but he bounds to the foot of the stairs and barks happily up at my mother.

'What *are* you doing, Rufus? Get back to your basket. Go on.'

The commotion allows me to crawl away into the kitchen, into Rufus's basket, the only way I know to get him back to sleep. *Get in!* I will the puzzled animal. *Get in!*

126

Rufus is a good sort, he doesn't mind sharing and curls up with me, a cosy squeeze, his breath in my ear, my hand scratching his head, soothing him back to sleep.

All's quiet again. I remove a paw from my mouth and carefully extricate myself from Rufus's embrace, slip softly out of the kitchen and work my way back to the handbag and find it zipped up back and front and down the middle – *blast!* If only it were lying open, a credit card could have tumbled out of its own accord. But here I am unzipping my mother's property and poking around in her personal things, *leaving fingerprints*, I realize, picturing myself in the dock of a public courtroom, strangers peering down at the little scoundrel, gazing sympathetically at my poor mother.

I'm clutching my mother's leather purse, fumbling with a stack of plastic cards. Angle them to the light and take your pick, as long as it's one authorized by her signature. Here's one that won't look so bad if caught. Pocket it, zip up the bag, lean it the way it was and return, step by step, to my room. Softly close the door and sit at my desk, cover the angle-poise lamp with a

T-shirt and under its muffled glow, place my mum's library card reverse side up and study her signature and start practising on a foolscap pad. When I feel I've mastered her loops and swirls, I'll sign the form and sneak down and replace the card.

In the morning I can barely look my mum in the eye. The consent form cries *shame!* in my pocket. I'm an absolute disgrace, but oddly calm. I'm tired after so little sleep, but buzzing. What choice did I have? If I said, *Mum, may I play against the refugees?*, she'd say no, your work comes first. It was either commit this dreadful crime, or kiss football goodbye. Stick to being a swot or *live!*

At school Heather and Tessa tease me unmercifully.

'Forging Mummy's signature, you naughty thing.'

'Serious offence, Sparrow.'

'You could be suspended.'

'Expelled!'

'Don't say that.'

'Arrested.'

'Taken into care.'

'You could go to jail.'

'Don't, please . . .'

'Go down for several years.'

'Banged up with dope-dealers and murderers.'

'Criminal record an' all.'

'*Please* . . .'

'Don't worry.' Heather pats me on the head. 'We'll visit ya.'

My eyes sting. Tess takes pity. 'Don't be daft, Lewis, we're only messing. I'll call your mum later, tell her we're working real hard together.' She winks.

'W-what if she w-wants to speak to me and I'm not there?'

'Don't worry, I'll think of something.'

twelve

All day I'm anxious about travelling in the minibus, packed in with Sir and all those yobs, some of them hating us, throwing me and Zulfi dark looks because we're threatening their places. Me, Lewis, threatening someone's place? *Ridiculous!* Don't they realize I'm petrified, my confidence evaporating like a pool on the African plain?

Talking of Africa, we're not in the minibus at all, but with Mrs Okocha, strapped in the back of her car. She's leading, since she arranged the outing and knows where we're going, and we can look back and make faces – Zulfi can, *I* daren't – at the minibus trying to keep up.

'How much further, miss?' asks Zulfi, who can't wait.

'Look!' she points.

Ahead we glimpse the sea crouched against the sky, dull grey and sprayed with white flecks like drool on Rufus's blanket. My heart trips at the thought of my dog. I miss him, I even wish I was home coaching Lindsay. Mum thinks I'm with Tessa. I wish I was.

We've arrived; we pull up outside a church. Someone stamping up and down in the cold is there to greet us – a thin pale vicar in jeans and dog collar, who shakes hands with Mrs Okocha and Sir, waves us boys a cheery hello and leads us into a hall where we're left to get changed. It's freezing. The others jostle for position around a solitary gas fire, leaving me and Zulfi in the cold. What am I doing here, my bare flesh exposed in this unfamiliar place, putting on the team's impressive maroon shirt, white shorts and striped socks and a pair of boots borrowed from Zulfi who has the same sandpiper's feet as me? Mangled by mud and rain, the boots are stiff and cracked and missing half their studs. They look funny on the ends of my milk-bottle legs; Charlie Chaplin turning out for Saley Marsh Middle School.

I suppose we were expecting a proper pitch and nets, but we find ourselves trooping down a lane to a public park where a few individuals are walking dogs and pushing buggies, and men speaking a foreign language are marking off a pitch with sticks for corner flags and sweaters for goalposts. As for the opposition, I confess I half-pictured a crew of Artful Dodgers with shredded scarves and blackened faces and am surprised they don't look all that different from us. In fact they don't look *any* different from us.

Their grown-ups shake hands with our grown-ups, and we shake hands with all of them, nervously, because they *are* different, they speak a funny language and come from far away and, as I watch, fascinated, I imagine I detect something pinched and haunted in their faces after all they've been through: the battles and burning houses, the dead bodies these boys must have seen, weeks and months hiding in frozen forests, the long snow-blown marches to safe borders. Yet they look happy, fooling together, laughing, kicking a couple of balls around and hardly noticing us. You can see they're closeknit and I've a feeling my teammates aren't aware of how tough this could be.

The opposition wear tracksuits, some shabby, some newish, all colours. I'm half-expecting them to strip off to reveal some classy Kosovan strip, but tracksuits are all they have, and decent enough boots, and now they're putting on brilliant red sashes which glint in the mist like open wounds.

Joey and Winston and the others are warming up and looking suitably cool and cocky.

'I'm looking forward to this, sir,' says Lee Jordan.

'Yeah, I can feel a goal or two in my boots today,' says *Slicker* Lunn.

'See if you can coax them out of your boots and into their net,' Sir remarks.

Zulfi and I sit out the first half, stand actually, hopping up and down and beating ourselves to keep warm. I didn't sleep last night and I'm worried I won't have any energy when my moment comes and I confess, watching Joey and Winston combining in a promising early move, that I'm willing them to play shockingly, so *I* won't look so bad later. When Winston Daley moments later fluffs a good chance, and Sir holds his head in agony, I'm secretly relieved.

Grown-ups are funny. While Sir patrols the invisible touchline like an army instructor, the opposition's coach, about Sir's age but leaner and moustachioed, watches impassively, smiling occasionally when one of his boys miskicks or falls over, like a man exercising his dogs in the park.

'How long h-have they been p-playing together, miss?' I enquire.

'About a year, Lewis,' says Mrs Okocha peering over the fake fur collar of her coat. 'They try and play every week.'

It shows. They move with speed and fluency, and then slow the game like professionals, and seem to control the ball effortlessly on the bumpy ground.

'They l-look like they could f-find each other in the dark, miss.'

'Yes, Lewis, they probably did when they were escaping.'

It's a bit embarrassing. The nearest we come to scoring is a fitful shot from Joey which flies harmlessly into a hedge, an attempt greeted by delirious shouts of *Goal!* from half the team.

'That was easily in, sir!' Joey and others surround the vicar-ref, jostling him like they do on telly.

'Too high, lads.'

'No it wasn't!'

'Clipped the top of the bar.'

'How do you know?' says Joey slyly, since the improvized goals have no crossbars.

'I *heard* it, son,' winks the ref.

By half-time we're fortunate to be only three–nil down. Mr Marvin gathers the team and tries to lift their spirits by telling them how useless they are. They hang their heads. Zulfi hovers hopefully.

'I can't believe what I'm seeing, after all the work we've done.'

'Don't look at me, sir.'

'I *am* looking at you, Jordan, or have you forgotten the purpose of passing is to find one of your own team, rather than *We mustn't hog the ball – here, you have it!*'

'Sir . . . ?' Zulfi stretching.

'And as for you, Spinx, you're meant to *shoot* at goal, not gaze at it like a flaming tourist attraction. Why not bring your camera next time, take a few shots of their grinning keeper!'

'*Sir . . . ?*' Zulfi straining for attention.

'And Daley, for pity's sake—' Poor Mr Marvin's really suffering. 'If you're going to take that long each time you shoot, why not ask them if they wouldn't mind going off for a cup of tea while you line yourself up . . . !'

'*Sir . . .*' Zulfi stretching his arm as high as it'll go.

'What *is it*, boy?'

'What about us? You promised!'

'What?'

'Oh, *sir*,' Joey groans, 'you're not serious about them?'

'This is a big boys' game today, sir,' Winston advises.

'We'll get massacred!' warns Lee Jordan.

'We're getting massacred already,' says Matthew Fallon, our wretched goalie.

Sir's waving everyone away, looking at Zulfi as if he's only just recognized him.

'Ah yes, the scorpion and the sparrow-hawk – where *is* the sparrowhawk? There you are, Overfeld. This should be interesting.'

There's no escape. I'm taking off my sweater, doing a few tragic stretches Tessa taught us. Zulfi grabs my hand, shakes it so hard he nearly dislocates my shoulder.

'This is it, man – this is *it*!'

The second half's underway and the pitch seems *huge*, the goals miles off, goalies blobs in the mist, and Zulfi's nowhere near. I'm on my own, shadowed – I've just noticed – by a huge fellow with dark brows and scars on his legs, stalking me like a tiger. I'm breathing too fast, my air cut short by the sea wind and sharp little flurries of nerves, and I'm thinking, *I can't do this, I can't* – while another voice spits, *You can, you must, you daren't fail now*.

But it's not that simple. The tiger is swift and sharp and easily cuts out the rare balls that come in my direction, and when one finally reaches me, he's on to me like an electric shock, nothing brutal, just a snappy tackle that robs me with embarrassing ease, drawing groans from my teammates. I feel hollow and defenceless. I keep running, looking eager, trying not to hear Sir's impatient yells, not to feel Joey and Winston's touchline scorn.

I must adapt, I tell myself, react quicker.

The goals keep going in at our end; we're being given a football lesson, not by Sir shouting himself purple, but by the skill and *rapport* of these war-children.

Time's running out, not so much for us – we're seven down already – but for me to *shine*. I can't bear the jeers and I'm beginning to loathe my ruthless marker. I'm sick of the sight of him, sick of being his prisoner. I want to break free, throw off my shackles and *live*!

With minutes to go my chance arrives: a shout from Zulfi – still running, eyes wild and hair streaming – a pass aimed for me, too neat perhaps, too obvious, because

Tiger's on to it, I can feel him coming like a thunderbolt – only he's not having it this time, this one's *mine*, I vow, and instead of waiting for it to reach me, I race to meet the ball with Tiger on my shoulder. Then instead of controlling it, as expected, I try something I've only done in daydreams – surprising my jailer by prodding the ball *away* from myself, skipping over his despairing tackle and leaving him stranded while I look up and float a ball not *to* Zulfi but into his computed path.

In the hall afterwards, as we're crowding round a table of refreshments, Tiger taps me on the shoulder and I catch my breath. What's he going to do, smack me round the hall?

'Hey, you play good,' he says, breaking into a smile.

'*Me?*' Amazed. 'Not r-really.'

'No, no, you play good.'

His eyes seem to be saying, *OK, you only beat me once, but you did it in style*.

My heart swells. Maybe I do have something others don't, an instinct for the unpredictable, the *amazing*.

Their keeper's nice too and gives Zulfi a thumb's-up.

'Good shot . . . best save I make for long time.'

It *was* a good save. Zulfi collected my hanging pass, set his sights and fired a stinging shot their keeper only stopped in a dazzling whir of limbs.

'You wake me up,' the keeper confesses. 'I was making a nice little dream.'

Thirteen

Sir's tight-lipped. Nothing he's seen today against the Kosovans has convinced him we're going to beat Broadstones or Pemberton Hall, whatever strike pair he fields. He must be having nightmares about Miss Proudfoot as I'm having day-mares about Mum because by the time Mrs Okocha drops Zulfi home and sets off with me for mine, it's seven-fifty, later than promised.

'Miss, d'you think you could d-drop me at the end of my s-street?'

'I'd rather see you to your door, Lewis, if you don't mind.'

'I'd p-prefer the end of my street.'

Intrigued. 'Why?'

I hesitate. I don't want to start lying to Mrs Okocha.

'Are you embarrassed to be seen with me, Lewis?'

140

Shocked, 'Oh n-no, miss, on the c-c-c—'
On the contrary, I want to say. *I'm proud to
be riding in your car, I really like you and I
still dream about your drama club.*

'What is it then? Your parents did sign
that form, didn't they? They must have; we
collected them all in.'

My silence alerts her.

'Lewis . . . ?'

'I'm s-sorry, miss.'

'Why, what have you done?'

I can't look at her. She pulls over,
switches off the engine. I meet her gaze.

'I've done something t-terrible, miss.'

'Tell me,' she says gently.

I'm afraid. She's my favourite teacher
and I don't want to lose her.

'I didn't think my m-mum would let me
go, s-so I . . .'

'Yes?'

'Well, I *knew* she w-wouldn't, so . . .'

'So you what, Lewis?'

'Forged it, miss.'

She looks at me, amazed. I obviously
don't look the type to commit such a crime.
She's rooting through a folder, finds my
form, holds it to the light.

'Well it looks genuine. You sure you
forged it?'

I nod, head bowed, bracing myself for a lecture – *You silly boy . . . Whatever were you thinking? . . . I'm really surprised at you.*

Instead I feel a finger lift my chin and I meet her calm grave eyes.

'Promise me never to do anything like this again – and I'll keep it secret.'

'I p-promise.'

She leaves me a few doors from the house and whispers, 'Good luck,' as if predicting I'm in for a storm anyway. How right she is. Soon as I enter the hall, I feel a chill in the air – no greeting from Rufus, no sign of Lindsay, Mum standing like marble.

'I'm s-sorry I'm late.'

'Did it go well with Tessa Hacket? How are the projects coming on?'

For a moment I'm taken in.

'It was r-really good, we got l-loads—'

Loads done, I was going to say, but now I see the look in her face, worse than anything before, like in Dickens when a boy's caught out and is in for a thrashing. She *knows*, somehow she knows. Tessa must have blown it, and if there was some way of leaving my body instantly and without too much pain and going to heaven with Boris, I'd take it.

'Where have you been?'

I weather her gaze. She's clutching a piece of paper. I know what it is – the top sheet of the pad I used to practise her signature, carelessly discarded in my bin.

'How dare you sign my name! That's a wicked thing to do. And how dare you lie to me—' Towering over me, shaking with anger. '– when you know it's the one thing I can't stand?'

I know, we all know, she's said it often enough. *Her* mother – my gran – must have drummed it into her because *she's* obsessed with it as well, says lying is the worst thing you can do to your parents. If I swore at Mum, it wouldn't be half as bad. I wish I could tell her I hate it too.

I feel awful about lying to you, Mum, I really do . . .

'I'm deeply disappointed. Get up to your room, and I expect to find you washed and teeth-brushed and tucked up in precisely five minutes, and for the next four weeks, young man, you'll be home by four and in bed by seven. Is that understood?'

Tail between my legs, I catch sight of Rufus peering mournfully from his basket as I scuttle upstairs and hurry past Lindsay's room where she's reading aloud

143

to herself, pretending to be OK when really she's upset, and I want to go in and say, *Look, I didn't mean this to happen, it's just that* . . . but I daren't do anything but slink into my room.

'I can't believe it, I really can't,' Mum calls up the stairs, 'after all we're doing for you and all the trouble your father took speaking to you. I'm frankly astounded – you wait till he hears about this!'

Don't you realize Daddy doesn't care? I want to tell her. *He'll back you up to keep you quiet, but all he ever thinks about is himself.*

I'm in bed in four minutes flat, facing the wall, heart pounding, eyes stinging, hating myself. *Don't you want to get on?* I ask myself. *Be successful one day, make money? Forget football, forget drama, get on with your work and stay out of trouble.*

Mum enters. I keep my eyes shut, praying she won't start again, longing for a soft hand on my cheek.

The light goes out and she's gone, footsteps fading.

In the morning, Mum barely speaks to me, Rufus keeps a low profile and Lindsay watches me over her cornflakes, wondering what's got into me, hoping the crisis is over, everything back to normal in the Overfeld kingdom – or queendom.

In school, I run into Tessa.

'I couldn't get you to come to the phone,' she shrugs, 'when you weren't there.'

'You s-said you'd th-think of something.'

I can't believe I'm standing up to her, criticizing her.

'Give me a break, Lewis. I said you were busy with the project, but your mum wouldn't listen and then, well, you know the rest.'

'I d-don't actually. We're not really s-speaking.'

'She drove over to get you – and you weren't there!'

I go round school so shocked by what's happened I hardly notice Joey and Jordan pouring scorn on me when I come into class.

'Look! It's Maradona!' points Joey.

'You and Malik, some strikeforce,' goes Jordan. 'Them Kosovans were shaking!'

'Yeah, shaking,' says *Slicker* Lunn.

'Oh shuddup,' says Winston spoiling the fun. 'We were just as bad.'

Joey looks daggers at his strike partner. 'Speak for yourself, Daley.'

'I am. I was brutal and so were you and

we better pray Sir doesn't drop us.'

The argument spreads but Zulfi keeps quiet. There's something secretive about him today, an aura of confidence. He says nothing until break.

'Guess what?' Drawing me aside. 'Sir smiled at me this morning.'

'Is that un-unusual, Zulf?'

'He's going to pick us, I'm telling you.'

'You th-think so?'

'Trust me.'

I look away. How do I tell him I'll never play football again? He frowns at me.

'Why you always such a misery guts?'

'I'm *not* a m-misery guts. I just have a p-problem mum. Last night was a n-nightmare.'

'Why, what did she do?'

I tell him everything. He's stunned.

'God, Lewis, I never thought . . .'

'It's my fault, you didn't f-force me.'

'Home at four and bed by seven for a whole month? Man, she can't do that! What about your rights? You should ring Anglesey International.'

He shakes his head pitifully, like I'm one of those convicts in chain-gang movies who they let out to break rocks in the heat of the day and return to cells at night.

146

'Thought you were going to stand up to her.'

I sigh miserably.

'Listen, Lewis, if you don't, you've had it, cos you're never going to grow up.'

'*Hmm.*'

'I mean it, man – you can't go on like this – you'll end up a grown-up wimp, still on Mummy's lead and Mummy going *Heel!* and *Sit!* You'll always be scared, man, scared, scared, *scared.*'

I nod gloomily.

'I'm thinking of me too, cos if you don't play, I don't get to play either. We're a pair, you and me, like Buzz and Woody, right? Superman and Robin, Samson and Delilah. You're just going to have to talk to her.'

'I s-suppose so.'

The very thought chills me, but before I get too shivery thinking about it, Oscar runs over looking even paler than usual, like he's seen the future and it's swarming with Lee Jordans.

'Mr Marvin wants you right away.'

'Oh, b-bad luck, Zulf,' I blurt, anxious for my friend.

'I think he's looking at you, Sparrow,' says Zulfi.

Oscar nods. 'Yes, he wants you, Lewis.'

'What have I d-done?'

'I don't know, but you'd better look out.'

It's a stone's throw from the playground, but it takes my petrified heart for ever to carry me up the short flight of steps and down the corridor to the classroom. Sir's waiting, legs apart, hands behind his back. If they hadn't got rid of corporal punishment, he'd be clutching a cane.

'Sit down,' he says, and I know by his voice I'm doomed – I can see the hangman's hood, the dangling rope.

'Practising for a career in counterfeiting are we, Overfeld? Fancy ourselves as a modern-day Uriah Heep?'

I gaze helplessly at him.

'I've just spoken to the principal. Your mother phoned. Seems you came with us yesterday under false pretences, involving both me and Mrs Okocha in your deception – thanks very much. The outcome, if you'd care to hear, is that your mother is taking you out of school.'

Out of school?

'Permanently!'

Permanently?

I blink, too shocked for breath.

'To say that she and Miss Proudfoot had words is the understatement of the year!

The row brought down power-lines for miles around and registered on the Richter Scale! Your mother intends sending you somewhere where irresponsible teachers don't distract children with pointless pastimes like football.'

Another school? My heart lurches sickeningly. All those new faces staring at me – the new boy, Lewis Overfeld, Lewis *who*?

'Dear God, I'll be sorry to lose you!' His tone softens. 'And I don't mean the team, I mean *you*, you're a good sort and an able student. Unfortunately you've brought it all down on your own head.'

'I'm s-sorry, sir.'

'Bit late for that, young man. Why didn't you tell me about your mother's feelings? I wouldn't have wasted my time and Mrs Okocha wouldn't have arranged that match specially for you and Malik.'

On cue, a knock. Mrs Okocha. 'Mr Marvin, I've just heard the news.'

'Don't look at me, Mrs Okocha. It's this young fool's fault that Miss Proudfoot's had an earful from his mother, I've had an earful from Miss Proudfoot and now Lewis is getting one from me. The whole thing's preposterous!'

'Your mother's obviously very upset,

Lewis,' says Mrs Okocha, 'and I'm wondering—'

'Bit late for wondering,' Sir interrupts. 'It's all decided – he's out!'

'Yes, but I'm still wondering—'

'She's taking him out at once. He's to collect his things, she's coming at two.'

I look at the clock. An hour left to save my life. 'S-sir?'

'*What?*'

'Could we h-hear what Mrs Okocha's w-wondering?'

'I was wondering if I should talk to your mother, Lewis—'

'I think you'll find her mind's made up,' says Sir.

'I'd like to speak to her anyway, if you don't mind, Mr Marvin.'

'*I* don't mind – but you'd better see Miss Proudfoot.'

'She's already agreed.'

When the others return to class after lunch, they find Zulfi and Oscar helping me pack.

'What's going on?' cries Tess. 'Lewis isn't really going, is he?'

Rumours have been flying. Everyone comes in and stares at me.

'I'm afraid so,' Sir replies.

'What, for forging a flaming signature?' Tess is as white as a sheet. Only yesterday she joked about me being expelled.

'Ask Miss Proudfoot, sir,' suggests Heather. 'Can't Sparrow run round the pitch ten times and do a million press-ups or something.'

'He's not being expelled, Jones, he's being punished by his own mother, pulled like a bad tooth – withdrawn, removed, extracted!'

'It's not right, sir,' cries Tess. 'He just wanted his chance in the team.'

'It's very wrong to falsify an official document,' says Sir gravely.

'Oh come on, sir,' cries Winston, 'it's not *that* wrong. He's not bullying kids or taking drugs.'

'And he's a good pupil, sir,' says Matthew Fallon. Friends I never knew I had.

'I agree, and if it were up to me I'd severely reprimand him and make him promise never to repeat such a thing, but it's not up to me so get out your readers and settle down.'

The silence is terrible, Zulfi and Oscar parceling up my books, me sweeping out my desk, everyone quietly reading, or pretending to, gazing at me, pitying me, despising me. I really am an outcast now.

'It's not fair, sir.' Tessa breaks the spell.

'Get on with your work, Hacket.'

'Well it's not, sir.'

'There are plenty of things in this life that aren't fair, young lady, but there's nothing we can do about it.'

Zulfi and Oscar return to their places. I sit, arms folded, staring out at the rain, my heart shrinking.

'There *is* something, sir,' announces Heather. 'We could all go on strike.'

'Yeah!' says Winston. 'Barricade the door, not let his mum in.'

'Thank you, Jones and Daley, for your invaluable contributions, and now if you wouldn't mind getting back to your readers.'

A car pulls up, heads crane to catch a glimpse of a woman striding into school under a wide umbrella, head high and shoulders out – a parent in pursuit of a delinquent son. We wait in silence. Small footsteps approach, a Year Seven messenger squeaks in the doorway. 'I'm to say Lewis's mum's here, Mr Marvin, sir.'

I shoulder my bags. I can't look at anyone, not even Zulfi.

'Bye, Lewis – good luck, Sparrow,' people murmur.

Sir walks me down the stairs, across the drizzling playground and down the corridor to the office where Miss Proudfoot and my mother stand like two haughty actresses waiting for the other to remember her lines. I hear myself scream, *How can you do this to me, in front of all my friends? I'm not a baby!* But of course I say nothing as Mum takes me by the hand and leads me out beneath her umbrella.

'Now don't worry, dear, it's all for the best,' she says, surprisingly calm, happy I suppose she's snatched me from the hands of these terrible teachers.

'It may seem a little drastic, but I've spoken to Dad and we're just going to have to tighten our belts, take less holidays, let Trudi, our cleaner, go, sell the car if we have to, and send you to a really good private school. Should have done it years ago.'

There's someone at the school gate, Mrs Okocha sheltering under a child's brolly. Mum hasn't seen her.

'Hello, Lewis . . .'

Mum jumps at the friendly greeting.

'Mrs Overfeld? I'm Mrs Okocha.' Offering her hand.

My mother looks at Mrs Okocha's outstretched hand and, fumbling with her bag and umbrella, manages to free a hand to return the handshake.

'Mrs Overfeld, if you could spare the time, I'd like to drop by later to—'

'Drop by? What for?'

'To say goodbye to—'

'You can say goodbye now, if you like.'

'I don't want to delay—'

'You're not delaying me. Lewis, say goodbye to Mrs Okocha.'

'Not here, Mrs Overfeld. We're very fond of Lewis at Saley Marsh and I want to say goodbye to him properly. It'll only take a minute. Would six o'clock be all right?'

'Well – I – I don't know—'

'Good, six o'clock then – bye!'

As Mum hunts for her keys, I watch Mrs Okocha walk back into the school I'll never see again, surprised at how easily she flustered my mum who normally flusters everyone else.

'The nerve of the woman,' says Mum as we drive off. 'People's manners nowadays – I mean *really* – and a teacher too. No wonder standards are sliding.'

I'm not listening. I'm watching the school dissolve in a wing mirror – a school I didn't always like but which now seems, as it vanishes, the most beautiful school in the world. Wasn't I just beginning to find my feet, beginning to be respected as an all-round boy, good at work and better than we thought at football, and beginning to be popular? I think there was sadness in the air as I left. I might have expected wise-cracks from Joey and Jordan but there wasn't a murmur. I didn't ask to leave. I don't want to leave. I want to say to Mum, *Couldn't you have said something? Couldn't we have discussed it?*

The rain beats the roof, we crawl in fuming traffic. Why does it have to be like this? Why is my mum lighting another cigarette and slapping the wheel with impatience? We can land space probes on Mars but can't manage simple manoeuvres on Earth without cursing. Cars are sup-posed to get you from A to B fast and make you happy but we're barely moving and everyone's miserable. I feel like bolting from the car, running off to Ruritania or Narnia or the Hundred Aker Wood where I could play all day and eat what I like and teach Christopher Robin bottle-top football.

Mrs Okocha's coming at six. What do I do

till then? Sit through another gloomy lecture from Mum?

The car's filling up with smoke. I open my window a fraction and breathe. My heart's a runaway train. I've been kidnapped by my own mother.

Thought you said you were going to stand up to her – Zulfi's voice in my ear – *or don't you want to grow up?*

At home, Rufus leaps to greet me and Mum, who usually says, *Rufus! get down, heel, boy – SIT!* says, 'Rufus, you silly old thing, control yourself. Look how thrilled he is to see you, dear. Go and get changed, pack away those school things in the cupboard and come down for some chocolate cake.'

'I don't want any c-cake, thank you.'

'Don't be silly, of course you do.'

'I'm not h-hungry.'

'You don't have to be hungry, dear, for chocolate cake. It's your favourite. I bought it specially, we'll have some together.'

'I don't w-want anything, but thanks anyway.'

'Then get changed, pack away your books and come down for a cosy little chat.'

The change in her tone frightens me. 'I've arranged for Aunt Sophie to collect

Lindsay and supervize her homework so we've plenty of time together, just the two of us.'

I don't want to pack away my Saley Marsh things – it'd be like burying them – and the last thing I want is a cosy little chat. As I climb to my room, a little flame of anger burns up in me. *I'm not standing for this. I won't be treated like a baby. You're right, Zulf, it's time to grow up.*

I place my bags before me on my desk and sit there in my school clothes. One bag's stuffed with textbooks, the other with a jumble of exercise books, pens, maths equipment, rough paper, stapler, hankies, energy store of nuts and raisins, paperclips, coloured felts, lunch-box, and grubby little Englebert – my toy mouse and good-luck charm who's helped me through so many assignments and tests and who lives in an old sock where the Lee Jordans of this world would never think to look.

'Are you coming down?'

Her voice makes me start. Half of me wants to call, *Just coming!* The other half hisses, *Don't move!*

Torn between obedience and mutiny, I sit at my desk gazing at the rain, thinking of Zulfi and Tess and the others getting down to arts and crafts, bustling round the classroom without me. I even miss Mr Marvin.

You're hopeless, Lewis – what are you?

H-hopeless, s-sir.

I smile at the memory.

'Lewis, where are you?' Mum repeats.

My heart pounds dismally, my stomach crawls with nerves, and though I tell myself, *You're crazy! Do as you're told!*, I'm strangely composed and refuse to answer.

'Lewis, are you coming, or what?'

I watch the sky, dense with rolling clouds, begin to clear.

My mother enters.

'Lewis . . .'

I don't move. I feel her at my back.

'Lewis, I'm speaking to you.'

I stare ahead, petrified.

'I thought I asked you to put away your things and get changed and come down.'

I really ought to say something, but I'm like a fish in a tank. I can move my mouth but I can't speak. I'm locked into silence.

'*Lewis!*' She's leaning over me, red-faced. 'What's the matter with you!'

What's the matter with me? I want to scream. *I hate you!*

'Get up this instant, put away your things and come down.'

I'm carved out of stone with a galloping heart. I couldn't move if I tried. I feel nothing. I *am* nothing.

'Lewis, you may not like what's happened, but I'm your mother and I decide what's best for you. Now I want you downstairs in precisely three minutes and we'll overlook this silly behaviour and everything will be fine – all right?'

She leaves. I gaze into space.

Minutes pass. I've never been more frightened – or more calm – in my life.

I hear her coming – *running!* – up the stairs, storming into the room.

'That's it, I've had it, I've absolutely *had* it. Either you do as you're told or I'm going to put you across my knee for the first time in your life and give you a really good spanking . . .'

My heart stops.

'Do – you – un – der – stand?' she cries, shaking with anger.

We remain, my mum and I, frozen in an odd sort of sculpture – me at my desk holding onto my bags, unable to speak or move, my mother bending over me, hands poised to seize me, unable to act.

She straightens – the spell is broken – and walks out.

I don't know how long I'm here – half an hour, an hour? – gazing into oblivion, afraid my mum will never speak to me again, afraid she'll wash her hands of me, but then I notice an odd sound coming from downstairs and as I listen, it sounds like Rufus whimpering in distress, and when I sneak out onto the landing and listen, I realize it *is* Rufus whimpering in distress. And now I can hear something else, something I've seldom heard and I've an awful feeling it's Mum, and as I tiptoe downstairs I realize it *is* Mum, bent over her work at the dining-table, crying, and that's why Rufus is crying.

She hears me and stops. I stand in the doorway, longing for her comfort, for her to say something that'll magic everything away. She feels me watching her, blows her nose noiselessly as only mothers can.

'Well, Lewis, I don't know what to say – I really don't.'

I can't tell if this is anger or bewilderment and stand shivering.

She turns to me, a baffled look, like a dog that's done its best and still can't get it right.

'Perhaps we could have some ch-choc-
olate cake?' I suggest.

'You have some, I'm not hungry.'

'You don't have to be h-hungry for ch-
chocolate cake.'

She looks tired and beaten. 'What I need
is a strong cup of tea.'

In the kitchen, while we wait for the
kettle, she folds her arms and looks at me.
'It's funny how one doesn't notice these
things,' she says mysteriously, 'the way
they just creep up on you. Perhaps I
preferred not to notice.'

She sips her tea and gazes away. I nibble
tasteless cake, trying to guess what she's
thinking. Perhaps she's going to send me
not only to another school but another
home as well. I'm going to be passed on like
an unruly dog to a family that can cope.

Mum steps into the hall to smoke a cigarette, because one of the few rules reserved
for grown-ups in this house is no smoking
in the kitchen. Of course the smoke drifts in
anyway. Smoke doesn't understand rules.

Then she disappears upstairs without a
word and my heart plunges. She's had
enough, she's packing her bags. What will
I tell the others?

Sorry, Dad, sorry, Lindsay, Mum's gone.

What do you mean, gone?

I upset her and she doesn't love me any more.

What! What did you do? Write off her car? Set fire to the house?

Normally I'd be doing my homework now but there isn't much point. Still it feels odd not doing it. I wish none of this had happened. Who needs football, who needs to shine? It wasn't so bad being a wimp, was it?

Mum returns with a new face, touched up in private.

A car pulls up. Steps approach – the bell rings. My mother answers the door. Mrs Okocha sounds too cheery. I'm afraid my mum won't like it but instead she invites my teacher in. We sit in the living room, Mum cool as you like, Mrs Okocha a little nervous, I think. She must have come prepared for slings and stones and here we sit over tea and scones, my mother coolly friendly.

'Thank you for seeing me,' Mrs Okocha's saying, 'it was all so sudden, the prospect of losing Lewis. He has his problems with teasing – sometimes malicious teasing, I believe – but on the whole he seems happy. Am I right, Lewis?'

162

'Mmm,' I agree.

'Lately he's been displaying hidden talents and we welcomed them. We had no idea how strongly you felt. We had no idea we were acting against your wishes. Would you prefer us to talk in private?'

Normally I'm banished when serious subjects are aired but my mother ignores the question as though it's of no consequence.

'Football's character-building, I'm told,' she says, 'but *I* haven't noticed. What I do see is all the time that's taken up with practice and matches and getting kicked black and blue . . .'

'I think it can help self-confidence,' Mrs Okocha replies, 'and drama certainly builds character and I *was* hoping, with your approval, that he might try for a part in a production of *Oliver!* I'm planning.'

'I don't believe this.' Mum pales. 'I agree to you coming round to say goodbye and here you are recruiting for your play!'

'Forgive my insensitivity, Mrs Overfeld. It's just that as a professional teacher I believe there's more to education than studying – more to Lewis than a conscientious pupil.'

'That's just my point. He *used* to be

conscientious. Now all he thinks about is football and it shows. Miss Proudfoot may pooh-pooh it but lately I've seen his ten-out-of-tens become eight-out-of-tens and his As become B-plusses, and it worries me.'

'I do understand, Mrs Overfeld—'

'I doubt it—' Mum stands suddenly, finds her cigarettes and fixes our visitor with a withering look. 'You've no idea how I worry day after day. He doesn't need football or computer games or whatever his friends get up to. It's a passport to the future he needs. I can't bear to think of him being distracted and falling by the wayside. It may all seem over the horizon to him now but life creeps up on us and suddenly it's too late to turn back the years . . .'

Lighting a cigarette, she takes a furious pull.

'*My* mother couldn't afford the materials or the books I needed. I never went to a decent school, I never became a painter or an architect and I'm determined that Lewis will stand tall one day, his pockets stuffed with qualifications. He'll go to the best university and get the best job and he'll thank me then, I promise you. Foot-ball, drama and friends can all wait, but his work won't wait and if he's unhappy now, it's so that he may be happy later.'

She turns her back and stares out of the window.

The silence is awful. I expect Mrs Okocha to slip away defeated but she's not finished.

'Mrs Overfeld, I've sons of my own, and the other day I caught my eldest smoking a cigarette and I was terribly upset because I want the same for them as you want for Lewis. We mothers are terrified of everything that could go wrong – they're going to fall behind, they're getting into bad company, they're sneaking out at lunch for junk food, they're going to flunk their exams and end up petty thieves instead of useful citizens, drug-dealers instead of doctors; they get flu, we think they're dying; they're glued to computer games, their brains will rot! They come home late – oh my God, there's been an accident! I *do* understand but I also know, Mrs Overfeld, that children need to – to breathe fresh air, to expand, to try new things. Don't you feel that, Lewis?'

Mrs Okocha's smiling urgently at me and all I can do is nod helplessly.

'Children need to stretch their wings and enjoy themselves,' she continues, 'if they're going to grow strong and healthy and confident, and worrying too much about them is not good for them. It gives them the wrong message.'

Mum spins round dramatically. 'Don't you think I know what's best for my own son?'

'With respect, Mrs Overfeld—'

'With respect, Mrs Okocha, his grades are slipping, you can't deny it. While he's having fun, others are overtaking him. I *won't* stand by and see him left behind. Now I think we'll leave it there, don't you?'

Mrs Okocha looks strangely pale, the glow washed from her skin. My mother extinguishes her cigarette and folds her arms.

'Perhaps Lewis would like to say something?' Mrs Okocha suggests a little desperately.

My mother looks at me. Returning her gaze I realize all my reserves of courage are spent. I want to back Mrs Okocha up but I'm afraid. *She* can go home now but *I* have to live with my mum.

Mrs Okocha stands over me, folds my hand in both of hers. 'Goodbye, Lewis, take care. Goodbye, Mrs Overfeld, thank you for seeing me.'

I hear my teacher's car fade into the rain and stand about confused while my mother says, 'Well, that's that. We'll call your father . . . see what he has to say.'

I still feel my teacher's presence in the room, hear the emotion in her voice. I mattered to her, I really did. I'm ashamed. I should have spoken up. She came round to support me and I did nothing to help myself.

Mum seems agitated. She keeps trying to reach Dad and he's not there. She wants his support, I suppose, wants to be sure she's doing the right thing.

I've no homework to do, no football training to look forward to, no drama club to dream about. I'm lost.

'Shall I take Rufus for a w-walk?'

Mum looks round. 'Don't worry, we're going to find you a really good school. Whatever it takes, whatever sacrifices.'

'Shall I t-take Rufus out?'

'Yes, do. No! It's pouring.'

'I don't m-mind, if he d-doesn't.'

'Well I do. I'm not having you getting soaked.'

'I'll take an u-umbrella.'

'I said, no. Do something useful. Read a book.'

'I n-need some air—'

'I said *no*!' she blazes. 'What's the matter with you? Do I have to say everything ten times. Do as you're told.'

Stunned into obedience, I stand head bowed. Then, without warning, I explode.

'*No!*'

'I beg your pardon?'

'I won't do as I'm t-told. I'm sick of doing as I'm t-told, tired of being good as g-gold, f-fed up with you r-running my life. It's *my* life t-too, and you're s-so unfair. I work r-really hard, I do really w-well, and even if my m-marks have slipped a bit lately, they're still p-pretty good—'

'Pretty good's not good enough, young man,' she shouts.

'It is!' I shout back. 'Ask Mr M-Marvin—'

'What does he know? He's only interested in football.'

'What d-do *you* know—?'

'How dare you speak to me like that?'

'I do d-dare, I do, I'm s-sick of it, sick, sick, s-sick of it . . .' I yell and run from the room, scattering poor Rufus who skids on the floor like a cartoon dog trying to get out of my way as I rush by.

I get undressed and into bed and turn out the light. My mother's whispering heatedly on the phone below, ringing round the family, drumming up support, I suppose. I don't know. I don't care. I hope she sends me away. I want new parents. I wish it was 1940 and they were sending me deep into the country to escape the planes – a simple merry farming family with a hay loft and a donkey and ducks in the yard. As long as I could take Rufus with me.

Late in the night I dream of a car in the rain, Dad driving home from some faraway place.

In the morning, I find it wasn't a dream. Lindsay has stayed over with Aunt Sophie and I'm faced with both my parents over the breakfast table. I'm not a huge fan of breakfast cereals at the best of times – all those gaudy packets and wacky flavours and silly offers – and today they taste even more like sugar-coated polystyrene.

Rufus sighs miserably in his basket. He hates bad atmospheres.

Mum looks exhausted. She hasn't slept. Dad looks bemused. He's good at *playing* families, but hopeless in a real one. I want to say to him, *Look, the battle's between me and Mum – there's nothing you can do.*

'Lewy,' he says softly, 'I think you should apologize to your mum . . . not for anything you said, but the way you said it. I know you were upset, but shouting at her . . . well, it's just not on.'

I can't apologize fast enough. 'I'm sorry, M-Mum, I didn't mean to sh-shout. It just c-came out.'

'I know,' she says coolly. 'I'm sorry too, I'm sorry *I* shouted. Let's agree not to shout any more. Let's agree to talk more instead.'

I gaze at her. She's smiling painfully. I'm not sure how this is going.

'I've been so busy, I haven't had time to listen to you. I want to listen to you now, whatever you have to say.'

I blink at her. Now that she's giving me an opportunity to speak, I'm tongue-tied.

'I'm listening, Lewis. What do you want to say? I mean, do you really believe you can fit in things like drama and football with all the rehearsals and training involved, and still pass your tests with top marks?'

'Mum, you t-talk as if the teachers at S-Saley Marsh are all s-sports fanatics and d-drama mad. They c-care about my work. It's their j-job to get me through exams. They want me to excel at s-sport *and* d-drama *and* exams. If only one h-half of me is educated, I'm like a bird with a c-clipped wing. They have f-faith in my ability. I need you and Dad to have f-faith too. I need you to . . . to . . . to c-celebrate *all* of me, not just the Lewis who's good at s-sums and c-comprehension.'

They gaze at me blearily over their coffees, Mum in her dressing-gown after cancelling her morning's appointments, Dad in his leather jacket, mobile phone twitching in his pocket, ready to call a cab and fly.

'Anything else?' Mum asks.

Her tone encourages me. She wants to understand . . . I think.

'W-well, yes, there is . . .'

Oh dear, what am I doing? What am I saying? I can't tell her this, she'll go mad.

'Well, go on.'

My mouth is dry. What I have to say is too shocking, but if I don't speak it'll be like Lee Jordan in the showers, only half-standing up to her, only half-solving the problem, half-growing up.

'Well, you see, I d-don't think it's only . . . I mean there are l-lots of other reasons why my marks c-could s-slip from time to time—'

'Such as?'

'Well, um, f-for instance . . . the t-teasing

Mrs Okocha mentioned, feelings of i-inferiority . . .' I don't know where to look. I stumble blindly on. 'And things outside s-school.'

'What do you mean, outside school?'

I look up, meet Mum's gaze. 'Things at h-home.'

'What are you saying?'

'I'm saying . . . I'm saying that . . . it's h-hard to c-concentrate if there's s-stuff at home . . . anxiety to do with un-un-fair expectations and over-p-protection. Some kids c-could be unhappy and p-parents be so concerned about their marks they don't n-notice.'

My mother stares at me. I'm afraid she's going to go off like a bomb. But when she speaks, there's a kind of pleading in her voice, soft and hurt.

'Do you feel over-protected . . . do I over-protect you . . . are you anxious . . . unhappy?'

Silently I return her gaze and watch as her eyes fill up. She looks away, sad, dazed, and I can't bear it. I want to throw my arms around her and say, *Don't worry, it's OK, you're the best mum in the world!*

Dad, looking uncomfortable without a script, pats Mum tenderly on the hand.

Mum finds a hankie, dabs her nose. 'I only want what's best for you, Lewis—'

'I know, M-mum—'

'I really do. And if it's best you stay in that school, if it's best you play football and do drama and whatever you need to do . . . then I give in . . .'

fourteen

There's a strained atmosphere in the house. Mum seems distant and I hate it. I hear her talking to Dad – heavy sighs and snatches of *I'm all right now – yes, I suppose so*, and then fiercely, *But how can we be sure we're not failing him?*

Perhaps she's having trouble forgiving me for defying her. Perhaps she needs to punish me for growing up. I suppose it's been a shock for her. A shock for me too. I can't eat, can't concentrate.

My mum doesn't love me any more and is planning to give me away.

Lindsay keeps whispering, 'What's up with Mum, she's so *weird*!'

I say, 'Ask her yourself.'

So she says, 'Mum, why are you so – so funny all the time?'

'Funny – what do you mean?'

'I don't know – quiet and, you know, *quiet*.'

'Don't be silly, I'm fine,' she laughs. 'Just a bit tired. Managing a challenging job, challenging children and a challenging husband, dog and cleaner is – well, *challenging!* But I'm getting used to it,' she adds.

'Getting used to *what?*' cries Lindsay.

'My children growing up and shouldering a little more of the responsibility.'

Next day, Dad's gone again and Mum does something she *never* does, keeps me and Lindsay off school and takes us to the zoo and buys us chips and ice cream, and it's almost fun and we nearly have a good time but the weather's wet and the animals look sad and Mum's cheeriness has a hollow ring.

I'm allowed to take one more idle empty twitchy day out *sick* and then return to school. The staff have been warned of my mum's conversion but pupils in corridors stop and point and when I walk into class everything hushes. They look at me like I'm a ghost and are tempted to touch me to make sure I'm real.

'He's back, sir,' Zulfi blurts.

'Your powers of observation never fail to amaze me, Malik.'

'You really back?' cries Tessa. 'Did your mum say it's OK?'

'Nah, he's run away!' says Heather.

'You missed us, Sparky, didn't you?' shouts Winston.

'Welcome back, young man,' Mr Marvin greets me. 'What about a speech?'

'I d-don't think so, s-sir.'

'Oh really, you're useless, Lewis – what are you?'

'I'm n-not useless, sir.'

'*What?* Not useless. What are you saying, boy?'

A timid grin. 'N-not any more, sir.'

'*Hooray!*' someone cheers, Tessa I think, and then everyone's on their feet clapping and cheering – laughing at me, with me, I'm not sure – even my enemies, the whole class stamping and cheering, banging desks and slapping me on the back.

Shocked, confused, happy.

'That's enough, thank you,' Sir calls above the hullabaloo. '*Thank you!* A little order please, this isn't—'

'– the House of Commons!' everyone cries delightedly.

Calm restored, Mr Marvin peers down at me.

'Well, aren't you sitting down, Lewis? Or

were you planning to take the class –
trained as a teacher while you were away?'

Everyone laughs and Zulfi and Oscar
take my bags and escort me back to my
empty place.

'Sir, can we have this period off to chat
and stuff?' suggests Heather.

'To celebrate, sir?' cries Tessa.

'*What?* No work?' says Sir, appalled.

'No work! no work!' chants the class.

A look from Sir quells us, and sticking
out his chest like a gent from Dickens, Mr
Marvin announces that anyone who even
thinks of doing any work will be severely
punished!

fifteen

The training's full on, lunch-times and twice a week after school. Mr Marvin's done his sums. We need at least one win against either Broadstones or Pemberton Hall – or we finish bottom of the table.

Zulfi's excited. I try and persuade him not to count his chickens, not to assume we're playing, but he says, 'Stuff the chickens – wait till they see they're up against a sparrowhawk and a scorpion!'

Training's hard. Miss Proudfoot's preying on Mr Marvin and Mr Marvin's preying on us.

'Malik, you clown, you've two feet, use them!'

'But sir, I'm useless with my left.'

'Then leave it at home. Overfeld! Call that a tackle – I've seen scarier poodles! Keep this up you two and you've as much chance of making the team as playing for England!'

Against Broadstones, Sir keeps faith with Joey and Winston, leaving us on the touch-line again, flapping about to keep warm. It's a comically scrappy game, so lacking in skill and guile that Sir is hoarse by half-time and delivers his furious notes in a whisper.

Broadstones are dour and defensive and, as the second half huffs and puffs in the dwindling light, it looks as if they're going to get their wretched draw and we're going to earn a futile point when Matthew *the Eagle* Fallon fluffs a simple save and lets the ball trickle under him. The ref looks at his watch, Mr Marvin does the same and yells at me and Zulfi to strip off and get on and *Score – twice!*

Joey and Winston troop off like exhausted roadrunners; Zulfi and I fill our lungs with icy air and run on with minutes to go. How can Zulfi look so eager, so sure of himself when there isn't time to warm up or wish each other luck?

We're on so fast I haven't even time to die of nerves. The wind cuts my cheeks and hands, I run here and there, inviting passes, looking lively, but I still haven't touched the ball when the ref blows a long cruel note. Even now Zulfi's rushing to tackle an opponent, unaware it's over.

Poor Mr Marvin's in a state, too shocked to burn our ears, too alarmed to do anything but glower. Tomorrow he'll have to face the wrath of Miss Proudfoot. *What? Lost to Broadstones? What on earth is going on, Mr Marvin? Never in the history of this school have we finished bottom – I will not allow it, do you hear!*

Letters go out to parents; team members are required to train *three* evenings a week. My mother reads the letter and signs it without a word. I feel dreadful – that look she gives me, as if to say *I've done my best . . . if you break a leg or fail your end of year tests and ruin your life, don't blame me!*

'I'm hoping he p-picks me for the final game,' I tell her, 'and I'm hoping he d-doesn't . . .'

She frowns. 'Why?'

'Because it's an important g-game and I'd hate to p-play badly.'

'I'm sure you'll play brilliantly,' she says and goes off to make dinner, leaving me wondering if she means it as I get out my books and prepare for a long homework stint to impress her.

The training's horrendous. Mr Marvin's lost faith in us and we feel it. Our heads are down and the more he shouts the worse we perform and the more he shouts.

Only Zulfi's morale remains high. He's like a candle no wind can blow out, running hard, springing through his press-ups, leading the charge round and round the field, every twig in his body crying, *Look, sir – I'm your man!*

Saturday arrives, our demoralized team boards the minibus, Zulfi and I climb in with Mrs Okocha and Miss Proudfoot brings up the rear in her Stone-Age saloon. Tailed by a hardcore of loyal parents, we set off on the grim five-mile drive to Pemberton Hall.

It's a grammar school; their boys are bigger than us, powerful individuals who look like they start the day with raw lion and whale milk.

'They won't look so cool when we get stuck into them!' says Zulfi.

'Don't be daft, Malik,' says Joey. 'There's

no way Sir's going to play pinpricks like you two against that lot.'

'If it's skill he wants, he'll pick us.'

'Dream on, Malik,' Jordan jeers. 'You think he'll risk blowing it all on a couple of fairies?'

Sir calls us round. 'Gentlemen, I don't care how you win today, but win you must. A draw is useless, maximum points imperative. Do you understand? Essential, critical and long overdue!'

As he speaks, he glances round. Miss Proudfoot is arriving to address us, in mackintosh and wellies, planting herself before us like a cross between Her Majesty the Queen and that Lord Kitchener chap whose posters followed faint hearts everywhere in 1914 warning YOUR COUNTRY – in this case, your middle school – NEEDS YOU!

'D-Day is upon us, boys, our last chance to avoid catastrophe. I'm sure you don't need reminding of Saley Marsh's great tradition, which sad to say now rests in your hands. Mr Marvin constantly assures me there's talent in this team but we haven't seen much of it lately, have we? If it's there lurking somewhere, then today's the day because, mark my words, I will not countenance defeat. I have no intention of announcing anything less than a splendid win at assembly on Monday.'

The referee is calling us. Miss Proudfoot, puffing wintry air, snaps out a final call to arms.

'Saley Marsh has done a great deal for you boys, and it's time you paid your dues. Your school has spared no effort to provide you with a first-rate education and I expect you to spare no effort in return, to run and keep running till you drop, to give everything you've got and *more*!'

The ref's getting impatient, something about *It'll be dark before we start!*

'Heads high, boys, chests out, you're playing for Saley Marsh – who are you playing for?'

'Saley Marsh, miss,' we drone.

'Now get out there, take the game by the scruff of the neck and *win*!'

Zulfi and I watch yet again from the wings, this time with Miss Proudfoot and a small army of parents bawling over our heads. I don't like the atmosphere, all this shouting and urging on, this mania for winning. Someone's got to come bottom of the league – why not us? I'm just grateful Mrs Okocha's here, calming me with her presence, consoling miserable Zulfi.

'Lewis, there's still one part I haven't filled in the school play. Why don't you come along and try?'

'Thanks, miss, I'll th-think about it.'

'Do you sing?'

'A b-bit.'

'Miss Scott's doing the music. She'd like to hear you.'

She would?

Pemberton Hall are *class*. They wouldn't be a match for our Kosovan friends but there's a superior air about them. They've finished second in the league; this result won't affect them and it's obvious they're just out to enjoy themselves and show us who's top dog.

Joey and Winston strain every limb and muscle but they're having a torrid time against the Hall's monstrous defenders. Our attack forces a save or two, our defence keeps the opposition out with legions of luck and the aid of a rattled post and no-one can honestly fault them except Sir and Miss Proudfoot, who look gravely disappointed by the nil–all half-time scoreline, and demand more, *more*, *MORE!* I've never seen two grimmer grown-ups.

My mind drifts. I used to daydream about my parents coming to watch me, cheering as I scored for Saley Marsh or Middlesbrough. I'm glad they're not here to see me hanging around doing nothing, wasting my Saturday afternoon when I could be doing something serious like hosting Barcelona in my bedroom.

Zulfi tugs Sir's sleeve, not a clever tactic.

'Stop it, Malik. If I need you, I'll call you.'

The second half follows in the muddy slogging footsteps of the first until, surprise-surprise, *Psycho* Jordan volleys home a corner, bringing radiant sunshine to Miss Proudfoot's face, desperate relief to Mr Marvin's. They turn to congratulate each other, smile ecstatically and nearly throw their arms around each other. Parents are punching the air, shaking each other by the hand – you'd think our humble outfit had just saved the world from an intergalactic attack. With scarcely fifteen minutes left, it really is possible we're going to rub Pemberton Hall's noses in the mud and rescue the season.

But the Hall's noses react quickly and the cheers have barely died down when a roar from the home crowd salutes an equalizer. Mr Marvin gapes in disbelief, like an officer on the D-Day beaches who suddenly realizes he's been hit and has almost certainly had it. Miss Proudfoot's still swanning, unaware her splendid school is nineteen minutes short of disaster.

Zulfi's nudging me.

'*Ouch*, what is it?'

'We're on!'

What? Oh my God! Sir's pulling me to my feet, bombarding me with instructions I can't take in, telling us how everything depends on us now, which I'd rather not hear.

My head reels, vision blurs. I'm trembling so hard the pitch is pitching, the crowd swaying, and there seem to be several identical Joeys and Winstons trooping off to feeble applause – so unfair because they tried so hard.

'Good luck, Zulfi, good luck, Lewis,' says Mrs Okocha, patting us tenderly.

Miss Proudfoot sways towards us like a rhino. 'It's down to you now, boys – don't fail me. I want goals, boys, what do I want?'

'Goals, miss!' Zulfi barks.

'Goals, m-miss,' I agree.

We're on! The sodden turf is sucking at my borrowed boots, the massiveness of the pitch fans out like a wilderness, Pemberton

Hall's goal is a distant signpost, a fishing net in the grass.

'This is the big one, man!' cries Zulfi, his confidence marvellous and insane. 'You and me, Sparks!' he grins fiendishly.

There's an air of desperation about us – not Zulfi and I, but the team. In a way we two can relax because, with so little time left to save a season, no-one can blame it all on us. Perhaps that's why I'm not as anxious as usual. Who cares anyway, all this fuss about a ball and a couple of crooked goalposts?

It's my job to make myself available and then get the ball to Zulfi but they're on to me quickly, the pitch is a fenland of puddles, and it's hard to do anything with the ball but whack it hopefully in Zulfi's direction. The one time I do get it through to him, he's so excited to score he fires miles wide and Mr Marvin howls like a wounded beast and turns away distraught.

One goal – that's all that's needed – one precious goal.

The referee's checking his watch, defeat looms, the ball rebounds this way and that and skittles once more over the water to me. One, two defenders close on me, and I attempt something I've only seen on telly

– Allesandro del Piero I think it was – feigning to run the ball north and all in one flick dragging it south through his own legs, leaving his markers marking air. Not something I ever expected to try in reality, so why I try now I've no idea, but it works, sort of, the ball going one way and then, as though tugged by an invisible string, sucked under me in the other direction. And all at once the Hall's defence is open! Zulfi is running wide to lose the last defender as I slide-rule the ball into his scurrying path, a pass drawn in my mind and executed on a paddy-field, hit fiercely to skip the rippling water and allow Zulfi to take it in his stride, scoop it onto dry land and start zigzagging wildly to beat his man, making the poor fellow dizzy, forcing him – as Zulfi peels off his shoulder and goes for goal – to fling out a reckless leg and send him flying— *Splash!*

While the ref sprints across pointing to the penalty spot as though drawing attention to a corpse, the offender raises his arms in innocence as if to say, *Wasn't me – he wrapped himself around my leg, ref, honest!*

His teammates accuse Zulfi of diving; the home crowd boos savagely; I'm disgusted!

If that wasn't a blatant foul, then Jack the Ripper was a saint and the Holocaust one big holiday camp. I'm so proud of Zulfi and furious with these cheating boys and parents.

But why are my teammates looking at me? What's going on?

The ref has banished everyone from the area and is waiting for us to take the kick. With Joey off the field, we've lost our captain and our specialist penalty-taker. In his distracted state, Mr Marvin hasn't appointed another one and everyone's looking at everyone else because no-one wants the responsibility – and now they're looking at me again, because so far I'm the only one who hasn't refused.

'Kenny . . .' I mumble, looking at *Slicker* Lunn.

'*Me?*' replies my cocky enemy, meek as a lamb.

'Lee . . .'

'No way,' replies the hero, folding his arms.

'Zulfi, you're good at them,' I plead.

Zulfi scratches his head. He dispatches penalties like missiles in the playground, but this isn't the playground.

The day has gone eerily quiet. I glance

189

over to take in Mrs Okocha raising herself on her toes, Miss Proudfoot planted like an oak, and Mr Marvin standing head bowed, fists joined in prayer, and I imagine Mum and Dad crossing their fingers behind their backs.

Someone offers me the ball and closes my hands around it. Someone else takes it back again, wipes the mud off it and returns it. *There, you have it!* they're saying, and you can feel their relief as they step away, leaving me with my unexploded bomb. We all know that whoever misses this kick is going to have to answer to the rest of the team, their parents, the school, Miss Proudfoot and undoubtedly to God as well.

'You can do it, Sparrow,' Zulfi whispers. 'I know you can.'

Others join the chorus of encouragement and the ref once again draws my attention to the spot. I follow the direction of his finger but it's not easy making out the worn sodden smudge, more seagulls' droppings than a painted spot.

I place the ball and look up. Their goalie's an immense chap, ten, twelve feet tall, handsome in a pretty boy's band kind of way, with a brave face and hair in his eyes – the sort who saves goals for breakfast and eats mud-caked footballs for tea. His wingspan is so vast – as he stretches to amaze me – that he can almost touch both uprights simultaneously and looks capable of uprooting them, snapping them in two and scratching his back.

The whole world is waiting for me. Well, that's a first, and I may as well enjoy it, because thirty seconds or so from now I will surely be the sorriest brat that ever lived.

The keeper's staring at me, trying to frighten me. I ought to tell him there's no need. I'm already scared out of my wits, numb to my knees, almost too scared to care. Imagine, an entire season's at stake! A school's reputation hanging on a single kick!

And who have they chosen for this honour? *Me!*

'You can do it, man.' Zulfi's voice reaches me through the haze.

The keeper holds my gaze, his hard eyes and cruel lips saying, *You haven't a hope, mate!*

I return his gaze nonchalantly, like one who's taken a thousand penalties and only missed once cos a pretty girl went by.

'Get on with it,' says the ref. 'My second hand's wearing out!'

I take two steps back – think better of it and take one forward and one to the side – think better again and return to where I started and take five, six, *nine* steps back, a veritable cricket run-up. I'm going to hit this ball so hard it's going to carry master Pop Star clean through his own net.

Actually, I'm not. I'm not going to blaze it and I'm not going to attempt to place either to his left or right, because those are the options every goalkeeper expects. If only I have the nerve I'm going to try something I once saw on telly but have only ever executed in my dreams, because the little floated lob, straight down the middle, is tricky and extremely risky. It's such a mischievous and rarely attempted penalty that, if you get it right, the goalkeeper's completely bamboozled and you're not only a hero but a wit as well, a penalty-taker of exceptional character. But if you fail, if the goalie reads your thoughts, stands his ground and catches it like a party balloon, you'll look as silly as a soldier with a water-pistol and be laughed off all the way home.

But the floated lob straight down the middle is precisely what my mathematical mind has computed. The risk of placing the ball left, multiplied by the risk of placing it right, divided by the dangers involved in a surprise lob . . .

Here goes.

I'm shaking, but not so much I can't stand straight. I take a deep breath, look the keeper once more in the eye and start my long run to celebrity or disgrace. I've placed the ball so far away it takes an age to reach it, and when I do, I arrive an awkward stride short, obliging me to stretch for it when I'd prefer to find it tucked under my feet, making me strain as I lift my boot when I'd rather a smooth rising swing. But it's too late to check, I'm a pilot with no runway left, and with a faint thud the ball's in motion, lifting towards the goal, lifting *over* the goal, surely? I've hit it too hard!

The keeper's in motion too, completely fooled, hurling himself to the right, convinced that's where the ball's going when actually it's still in the air, an air balloon with hardly any wind behind it, catching a ray of sun as it hangs a minute, teasing me it's going over, teasing me again by threatening to hit the crossbar, when all the time it's dipping gently, landing with a soft *plop* and coming to rest in the long grass in the crook of the net.

For a moment there's utter silence. No-one is quite sure what's happened. The player was seen to take the kick, the keeper was seen to dive, but where's the flaming ball?

The keeper smashes his fist in the mud in frustration, the ref blows to signal the goal and screams go up all round me. My teammates swarm, I'm flung to the ground and buried – nearly drowned – under writhing bodies.

Sir is running on, waving and shouting, 'Get back, you fools! It's not over yet.'

I'm in heaven. I keep running with tremendous enthusiasm but I'm not really here. I've just scored a goal for my school. Me. *Me!*

Pemberton Hall come at us like wolf-hounds, but with Miss Proudfoot at our backs like the flames of hell, we tackle like demons – even I get in on the carnage – and before we know, the whistle's gone and they're carrying me from the field, tossing me in the air.

'What about Zulfi?' I cry. 'He made the goal.'

They drop me and run to him, lift him high on their shoulders. Even Joey and Winston are clapping; even *Psycho* Jordan, his face a weird mismatch of spite and delight.

The sea parts for Miss Proudfoot who summons Zulfi and I with a curling finger.

'Well, well, well,' she booms, grabbing us like a pair of thieves, 'you two were marvellous, absolutely marvellous! Thanks to you and Mr Marvin and all you boys . . .' beaming all around, 'the reputation of Saley Marsh is secure. You've made a silly old woman very very happy.'

Parents applaud, Mr Marvin pulls Zulfi and I aside and whispers, 'If you two clowns were my own sons, I couldn't be any happier than I am right now!'

'Thank you, sir,' I say, 'but shouldn't we go and shake their hands?'

'What? Oh yes, good point. Come on, everyone!' he calls, 'where are your manners?'

It's only when we're climbing back into the car and a breathless Zulfi tentatively points it out that I realize I've been talking without stammering. *Have I?* I look at him, not daring to speak in case it's true and I frighten it away.

Mrs Okocha drives in great excitement. 'I'm so proud of you boys, so terribly proud.' As we drive she asks me how I feel and I

daren't reply. She thinks I haven't heard
and asks again, and still I won't speak.
Finally she catches my eye in the mirror
and says, 'Come in, Jupiter, this is Earth
calling!' and I have to smile. 'How are you
feeling, Lewis, after your great triumph?'

'F-fine, miss, I'm f-feeling fine.'

Zulfi meets my sorry gaze.

sixteen

Mrs Okocha drops me home.

'Well done, Lewis, you were magnificent.'

I wave as she drives away. Zulfi waves out of the rear window, giving me frantic thumbs-ups to say, *We did it – we did it!*

I long to run in and cry, *Mum, Mum, I just scored the most important goal in Saley Marsh's history!* but the car's not there. She must be out shopping with Lindsay, and anyway, who cares?

My two worlds of school and home are drifting apart like icebergs.

Rufus hasn't hopped up drooling at the window at the sound of the car, so he must be out shopping too. I'm returning in glory to an empty house.

Once inside however, I realize I'm not alone. Someone's there; the TV's on, and for a moment I'm afraid it's a burglar watching telly while he works. My heart thumps and

I'm wondering, should I tell him *I think you've got the wrong house* when I remember mention of Dad coming home for the weekend, and there he is, sprawled in his armchair watching that phony wrestling he loves.

I stand in the hall, unnoticed in my muddy kit.

'Hey!' he says at last. 'Look at you, come here!'

He hops up and, smelling of tobacco, gives me a clumsy hug.

'I've got something for you in my bag – I'll get it in a sec. What have you been up to?'

'Playing f-football . . . for the school.'

'Excellent chap! But look at this, sit down, this is terrific, Hammerhead Hector and Igor the Tsar—'

'Playing for S-Saley Marsh, Dad.'

'You'll love it! Look! A Scots giant tangling with a Ukranian gorilla – terrific acting, isn't it! Laurence Olivier must be swivelling in his grave! Sit down, sit down!'

'D-Dad—'

'Honest to goodness, these guys should get Oscars.'

'Can I t-tell you something . . . ?'

'Sit down, sit down, relax.'

I flop down, gazing at Dad's programme,

depressed and angry. I want to turn his programme off.

'Don't worry, you can get cleaned up in a minute, they won't be back for ages, relax.'

Does he ever listen? Does he listen to Mum? Does he listen to his fellow actors or does he only hear his cues?

'Great stuff isn't it? *Ooh!* Did you see that? That must have hurt. Nah, 'course not, that's their art, you see, that's— *Hey!* What are you doing? Lewis? *Lewis!* I'm watching that!'

I've done it. I switched it off. I turn to face him.

'Something important h-happened today and I w-wanted to tell you but you never *ever* listen . . .'

In the quiet of my room, still in my muddy things, I get out my bottle-tops, but it's hopeless, I'm too upset, Middlesbrough are dire, Dynamo Kiev even worse.

A knock on the door. Ignore it.

Dad enters sheepishly. 'Can I come in?'

'I think that should be *m-may*?'

'Sorry? Oh yes, *may* I come in?'

I nod. He stands with his hands in his pockets.

'Listen, Lewis, I'm so sorry – you had something important to tell me and I was too busy watching rubbish and . . . do I really never listen? That's terrible.'

He's not acting. I think he means it.

'My dad didn't listen much either, come to think of it. Now I'm doing it. I'm sorry. What was it you wanted to tell me?'

'It's OK, n-nothing important.'

'But it was – you said so.'

I don't really want to tell him now, but he looks so lost, so keen to make it up to me. I tell him.

'You played for the school . . . and scored the winning goal . . . a penalty no-one else would take . . . ? Lewis . . . that's absolutely fantastic!' He wants to hug me, but thinks better of it and shakes his head in happy disbelief. 'There's nothing for it, we're going to have to celebrate! Go to a game together, grab a bite somewhere, what do you say?'

He really is pleased, too pleased.

Lying in the bath I'm depressed again. Why does it take a silly goal in a silly game of football to make my dad notice me? And also, why does the football season have to end just when I hit the big time? And also, why did my stammer leave me for a while this afternoon only to return after the game?

I hear the car, all the greetings downstairs, and then a hush.

I'm dripping wet when she puts her head round the door, studying me with a mother's eye.

She comes in and puts her arms around me. 'I'm thrilled, darling, absolutely thrilled.'

Me too.

seventeen

Back in school, I'm a star, everyone showering me with warm laughing praise – Tess, Heather, lads who didn't want me in the team, kids I've never spoken to – just as I always dreamed.

Zulfi's a star too, grinning like a fool.

Mr Marvin tries to be as strict with us as before but he really likes us now, me and Zulfi. We saved his bacon!

As the days go by, things return to normal. I'm still teased, more than ever, but it's harmless now, the nastiness has gone. No-one will ever bully me again – not because I scored a goal but because I've changed. I've grown up a bit, I'm more confident, I won't be pushed around any more. I'm not in with the in-crowd, but I'm not on the outside any more. Joey and Lee

Jordan look at me kind of funny but I'm not scared of them. This is the new Lewis, frightened of nothing!

Until Mrs Okocha startles me in the corridor.

'Lewis, I took the liberty of phoning your mum. I wanted to check if it's OK you audition for *Oliver!* and – guess what? – she thinks it's a good idea. So, my boy, I want to see you, bright-eyed and bushy-tailed in my room after school. And that's an order!'

Now I *am* scared.

I make my way to her room, hoping it's a silent part she has in mind, a pickpocket with his tongue cut out. Imagine me stammering all over the stage, people stifling laughs and fellow actors having to wait each time for me to finish.

'Hello, have you come about the drama?' Mrs Okocha teases. 'Don't be shy.'

I walk in, trying not to blush.

'I've auditioned a number of boys, *and* girls, for the lead, but no-one quite fits, and all the time I'm thinking, *Lewis would be perfect for it – Lewis IS Oliver.*'

She's joking, of course. She's going to say,

Don't worry, I'm only teasing, I want you to play an urchin, a messenger boy, the back end of a horse.

'Here,' she says, handing me the script. 'Try the lines I've marked.'

I look down at Oliver's lines. 'But miss, I c-can't do O-Oliver like this.'

'Why shouldn't Oliver have a stammer? I rather like the idea.'

I look down. The first line she's marked is simple enough. 'You sure it'll be O-OK?'

'Quite sure.'

I take a breath and think of the poor hungry lad and pipe up, *'Please, sir, may I have some more?'*

Mrs Okocha wrinkles up her nose. Was I that bad?

'Again, same line.'

Once more I hold up an imaginary bowl and cry, *'Please, sir, may I have some more?'* my voice clear and steady.

I lift my eyes to meet Mrs Okocha's gaze. She's frowning most peculiarly as though I just delivered the line in Hungarian.

'Try a different line.'

I try another line, and another and they all come out clearly and smoothly.

She's gazing at me – I've disappointed her.

'You're not stammering.'

'I'm s-sorry, miss. C-come to think of it, I didn't all the time I was on the f-football field on S-Saturday either.'

'Not stammering playing Oliver, not stammering playing football. Interesting, don't you think?'

'*Mmm.*'

'I wonder why?'

'Maybe I f-forgot . . . in all the e-excitement.'

'And what about Oliver?'

'Well, *he* doesn't have a s-stammer, miss, does he?'

'You know something . . .' resting a hand on my shoulder, 'soon I don't think you'll need that silly old stammer any more.'

'But you said you w-wanted it for Oliver.'

'Yes, why not? Try that first line again, with the stammer *in.*'

Another breath to get me into role and holding up the bowl I say, '*Please, sir, may I have some more?*'

Mrs Okocha looks at my face and bursts

out laughing. I tried to put it in and it wouldn't come!

She's smiling happily. 'This is going to be such fun.'

'Miss, you sure it's OK *without* the s-stammer?'

'Definitely, Lewis, no doubt about it!'

THE END

JOEY PIGZA SWALLOWED THE KEY
by Jack Gantos

'I think my brain is filled with bees.'

Joey is a good kid, maybe even a great kid, but he's always buzzing. As unpredictable as an unexploded bomb, he ricochets round the kitchen and spins down the school hall. He sharpens his finger in the pencil-sharperner and swallows his house key. He can't sit still for more than a minute – Joey is *wired*!

Told from Joey's own unique viewpoint by acclaimed American author Jack Gantos, this is an exceptionally funny and touching story.

'Funny, sad and very moving' *Jacqueline Wilson*

'Its wit, verve and strong story make it a fascinating read' *TES*

'An extraordinary book: moving, intensely funny and wonderfully enlightening' *English and Media magazine*

0 440 86433X

DEFENDERS
by Paul May

'Who wants to watch other people score all the goals?'

Chris is a goalscorer – but his life is a mess. He's falling out with everyone: his dad, his teachers, even his best mate. The only thing that makes him feel good is banging the ball into the back of the net. He certainly doesn't want to play in defence – even if his school team *does* need defenders . . .

Ian Rawson is Chris's new neighbour. An ex-Premier League defender, he's absolute magic on the pitch, in total control of the game . . .

When Chris sees Ian play, he starts to wonder. Has he got it all wrong about defenders? And if he changes his mind, will there still be a place for him in the team?

A terrific, action-packed soccer story from the author of *Troublemakers*, which was shortlisted for the Branford Boase Award.

0 440 864429

All Transworld titles are available by post from:

Bookpost, PO Box 29, Douglas, Isle of Man, IM99 1BQ

Credit cards accepted. Please telephone 01624 836000,
fax 01624 837033, Internet http://www.bookpost.co.uk
or e-mail: bookshop@enterprise.net for details

Free postage and packing in the UK. Overseas customers:
allow £1 per book (paperbacks) and £3 per book (hardbacks)